"You'll protect me from what's in the dark."

She smiled up into his face.

Damn, if he took so much as a breath, he'd be brushing up against her. How could one small woman unnerve him like this? She was too close. Much too close.

Much too desirable.

He tried to get a grip. "How about if what's in the dark is me?"

Her pulse began to accelerate. Things were happening inside her, things she couldn't stop. It was as if someone had thrown a switch. Or taken off her blinders.

Her breath backed up into her lungs. The words came out in a whisper. "I don't need protecting from you."

Unable to help himself, he ran his thumb along her lower lip. "I wouldn't be too sure of that."

Dear Reader,

This story should have been the third and last installment of THE DOCTORS PULASKI. But once I began writing about the family, two more sisters appeared. So this book is now only the middle one. You know what they say about the middle of the sandwich—it's the best part. I will leave that decision up to you, meaning you have to read the next two to compare.

In her own way, Leokadia, Kady for short, is my favorite sister. I named her after my mother (who absolutely hated her name and was appalled when I gave it to my daughter as a middle name). Writing about the Pulaski family is a wonderful treat for me because it brings back my childhood. Many touches from growing up Polish in New York City have found their way onto these pages. Kady is very outgoing. The hero, Byron, her protector-against-his-will, is not. There's a lot of my husband in him.

I hope this story succeeds in entertaining you. As ever, I wish you someone to love who loves you back.

Marie Ferrarella

MARIE FERRARELLA

Her Sworn Protector

Silhouette®
Romantic
SUSPENSE

SILHOUETTE BOOKS

ISBN-13: 978-0-373-27561-8
ISBN-10:   0-373-27561-7

HER SWORN PROTECTOR

Copyright © 2007 by Marie Rydzynski-Ferrarella

Visit Silhouette Books at www.eHarlequin.com

Printed in U.S.A.

Books by Marie Ferrarella

Silhouette Romantic Suspense

Silhouette Special Edition

MARIE FERRARELLA

This *USA TODAY* bestselling and RITA® Award-winning author has written over 150 novels for Silhouette Books, some under the name Marie Nicole. Her romances are beloved by fans worldwide.

To Bobbie Cimo, with deep affection,
for being so entertaining.

Chapter 1

There were times, like now, as she tried to get comfortable against the soft black leather seat of the limo, that Dr. Leokadia Pulaski felt she might have chosen the wrong field to give her heart and soul to. If she'd been a dermatologist, there would be no midnight calls rousing her out of sleep, forcing her to jolt her mind awake as she haphazardly pulled clothes on her body and tried to retrieve the directions to Patience Memorial Hospital out of her fogenshrouded brain. To Kady's knowledge, no one ever placed an emergency call before dawn because a pimple had made a sudden, unscheduled and drastic appearance.

But they did with cardiologists.

Exhausted as she was, feeling as if she'd been run over by two tractor trailers, the thought of changing fields, of leaving cardiology and her heart—no pun intended—was tempting.

Yet there was absolutely nothing in the world like the high she sustained when she managed to save someone's life. Or the feeling of accomplishment that arose by putting someone on the path that would steer him or her away from that dreaded midnight call and that life-threatening, searing pain.

Kady knew she was exactly what she wanted to be. A cardiologist associated with a top-ranked New York hospital. The same hospital where her two older sisters, Sasha and Natalya, practiced. She was good at what she did and she was proud of it.

Kady hung on to that thought as she sat in the back of the elegant stretch limousine that wove its way like a determined bullet through the just-post-dawn traffic. Its destination—the Plageanos Building where Milos Plageanos, the shipping magnate, had his penthouse apartment.

"Coffee, Doctor?"

The words rumbled out of the mouth of the dark-haired man sitting opposite her. The man who had been sent to bring her back. Tall, close to stone-faced, the black overcoat he had on strained against muscles that were a prerequisite in his line of work.

She only knew him by one name. Byron. Whether that was his first or last, she had no idea.

As far as Milos was concerned, Byron's job was to guard his body and to fetch his cardiologist on those occasions when his breath became short and his chest felt as if it was constricting.

They—she, Milos and Byron—had met in the emergency room two years ago when Byron had rushed in, carrying his employer in his arms. Milos had had a minor TIA, which amounted to a misunderstanding between his veins and his heart. The man had been at a club located two and a half blocks from the hospital. Something one of the ladies in his company had suggested, or possibly done, had resulted in the sudden need for medical attention. Byron had been vague about that when she'd asked.

Kady had been on duty that night, and when the nurse had pointed her out to him, Byron had been quick to commandeer her. She'd assessed the situation and had Milos feeling "good as new—better even" according to his own words within a couple of hours. Grateful and somewhat smitten, Milos had tried to hire her as his personal physician.

She had turned him down gently and found herself besieged with flowers, cards and gifts, all of which she sent back with thanks. As was his hallmark, Milos continued to be persistent. Eventually a compromise was struck.

Like all the physicians of her generation, Kady did not make house calls. Patients who found themselves in sudden need of her services met her in the emergency room of Patience Memorial Hospital. But Milos Plageanos was not the average patient. There had never been anything average about the man. Born to wealth, he had carefully overseen his inheritance until the name Plageanos became synonymous with the top shipping empire in the world. In the past forty years, there had been many challenges for the title. So far, only one had come close, causing a bitter rivalry to rage.

Milos was accustomed to putting a price on everything and was in turn surprised, annoyed and then greatly impressed when she turned down his lucrative offer. But he had not gotten to his present position in life by taking no for an answer. Accepting that she wouldn't be his personal physician, he still wanted her services whenever he felt he needed them. Since money in her own pocket didn't sway her, Milos decided to get to her by way of her generous heart. He informed her that he was donating enough money to Patience Memorial Hospital to build a new pediatric-cardiology wing, something he'd learned was dear to her heart. As if that wasn't enough, he also donated liberally to the free medical clinic where she and her sisters volunteered once a week.

"I am a man no one turns down completely," he

had proudly informed her when she came to thank him for his generosity.

Delivered by anyone else, the words would have made her balk. But aside from being shrewd and canny when it came to investments, when he wanted to, Milos could be very charming.

"A beautiful woman always brings that out in me," he had confided as he had kissed her hand, sealing their bargain. It was understood that he would continue making donations to the clinic so long as he could count on her to come when he needed her. Because the clinic needed so much in the way of equipment and supplies, she had no choice but to agree.

To his credit, he didn't abuse their bargain. In two years she'd only been summoned to his bedside twice. This made number three.

"Thank you," she murmured, taking the fine china cup that Byron offered. Milos believed in nothing but the best. She had no doubt that the cup was probably worth one week's pay at the hospital.

Kady took her coffee black, no cream, no sugar. Nothing to detract from the actual purpose of the drink.

Two sips later, Kady felt as if her mind was getting back into focus. She'd spent a good part of the night in the E.R., attending Wanda Kessler.

According to Wanda's husband, she had taken herself off her medication. Lucky for Mrs. Kessler, the woman had only had a minor heart attack. Just enough to put the fear of mortality into her.

After doing a thorough workup on her, Kady had signed the woman in overnight for further observation. Leaving the hospital, she'd just gotten in and dropped facedown on her bed in the apartment she shared with two of her sisters, Natalya and Tatania—now that Sasha had gotten married—when her cell phone had started to ring. For the space of a minute, she'd had an overwhelming desire to ignore it, but she didn't. She never did.

Bringing the cell phone close to her, she'd mumbled hello only to hear Byron's deep, authoritative voice rumbling in her ear. She knew what that meant. He was on his way to get her.

Kady barely had time to get off the bed and put her shoes back on before Byron was at the door. She'd stumbled out the door, asking questions about Milos's condition. He'd responded by saying that was what she was for, to assess the man's condition. Byron had helped her on with her coat as they made their way to the elevator. She remembered thinking that for a large man, he had a very light touch.

"How is he?" she asked again once the coffee became part of her system.

Byron was a man of few words, most of them noncommittal. Technically, she'd known him for two years and still knew nothing beyond what she saw, which, while very easy on the eyes and very pleasing, didn't satisfy her need to know.

"He wants to see you," Byron replied.

She suppressed an annoyed sigh. "That's not answering my question."

His wide shoulders rose and fell in a vague movement. Rather than look away, his deep blue eyes met hers. "I'm not the doctor, you are."

They were playing games, and this morning, she wasn't in the mood for it. While she appreciated Milos's generosity, she didn't like the idea of being regarded as a puppet. He pulled the string; she danced. The image didn't appeal to her.

"You know, maybe Mr. Plageanos should have a doctor on staff," she suggested.

Byron looked mildly amused. "He offered you the job but you wouldn't take it."

And she still wouldn't. To her, being a doctor had never been about the money, it had been about the helping. About the good she could do. And about the fact that Mama was very proud of having so many doctors in the family. The last thought made her smile.

"I'm not the only cardiologist in New York."

Byron regarded her for a long moment. In his experience, she was a rarity. A beautiful woman who didn't try to use her looks for gain. Most women in her position would have had some kind of arrangement with Plageanos that did more than repair faulty wiring and buy X-ray machines for a Spanish Harlem clinic.

"You know Mr. Plageanos. He wants what he wants and nothing else will do." His lips moved into a slight smile. It was all she'd ever seen him capable of. "He's paying you a big compliment."

She knew that in Milos's mind, wanting her for his personal doctor was the ultimate compliment. "I appreciate that. But being a one-patient doctor is not the way I see my life going. Mr. Plageanos can afford to have anyone he wants attending him." She thought of the clinic, of the defensive, frightened faces she came across almost every time she went. There was so much anger there, so much resentment at the world that had coldly passed them by. Charity seemed like just that: charity. "A lot of people can't even afford to buy aspirin."

His expression gave nothing away. "Not going to get rich that way, Doc."

To which she smiled and shook her head. He was wrong there. "There are a lot of definitions of rich, Byron."

Byron merely nodded his dark head. Crossing his ankle over his thigh, he sat taking quiet measure of her.

She felt as if she was under a microscope. What was he thinking about her? she couldn't help wondering. She decided to turn the tables on him.

"What about you?" she asked, edging closer on

her seat. "Don't you want to do anything different with your life than be at Mr. Plageanos's beck and call?"

"I've done 'different,'" he told her, his tone dismissing whatever that "different" entailed. "This suits me fine."

He paused for a moment, and she had the feeling he was debating saying something more. But whatever it was, she never got to hear it because he didn't open his mouth.

And then, before she could try to coax anything further from him, they were pulling up before the massive structure that Milos had put his name to when he bought the apartment building.

Each time she saw the building, a monument to the marriage of glass and steel, she was that much more impressed. And that much happier that she'd grown up in her parents' small two-story house in Queens. The forty-two-story building was a testimony to Milos's taste and his money. The lobby boasted original paintings from Milos's private collection. Nonetheless, it felt cold, distant.

They stepped into the elevator, and Byron pressed for the penthouse apartment. Kady swallowed twice, equalizing the pressure in her ears, before they reached their destination.

A white marble floor stretched out before them when the elevator doors finally opened. Waiting for her to get out first, Byron shortened his stride to match hers.

"I'd need a road map just to find my way around," she murmured, still as overwhelmed by the layout as she had been the first time she'd been brought here.

"You get used to it," Byron replied with a dismissive shrug.

The way he said it had her wondering. "Do you live on the premises?" Her words mingled with the echo of her heels on the marble floor. It had a mournful sound about it.

Byron looked down at her before answering. "Mr. Plageanos likes his people close by."

Close was not a word she would have associated with the premises. God only knew how many people could actually live within the structure without once bumping into one another. "Doesn't your wife mind not having a place of her own?"

She thought she heard a slight sound, something akin to a short laugh, escape his lips. "She might. If I still had one."

Still. Which meant he'd had one once. Kady pressed her lips together. She'd done it again. Even though she tried to curb it, she had a habit of probing; she always had. Her father had told her more than once that it would get her in trouble one day.

"It is good to having a mind that asks question," he'd said in his heavily accented voice. "Not always so good to having a mouth that is doing the same thing."

As usual, her father was right. Kady was about to apologize but didn't get the chance to follow through. They'd reached Milos's bedroom and Byron was knocking on the ornate door. The next moment, she heard a faint voice telling them to come in.

The room and the bed dwarfed him. Milos was not a little man in any sense of the word, but he appeared so in the custom-made double-king-size bed placed in a room that looked as if it could comfortably hold the population of a small third-world country. A giant hulk of a man she recognized as Milos's other bodyguard, Ari, was standing quietly off to one side.

"You should have been here sooner," Milos told her. A giant paw of a hand was dramatically placed over his heart. He tightened his fingers around it. "I didn't think I could hold on until you came."

Kady came forward, smiling at him, aware of the game. "And yet, you did." Her smile deepened as she assessed his color and the way he drew air into his lungs. Both were favorable. "I'm very glad."

Milos's eyes shifted to the man behind her. "That makes two of us. Maybe three, eh, Byron?"

"Yes, Milos," Byron acknowledged.

"All right." Kady set her medical bag down on the oversize nightstand and opened it. "Tell me what you feel, Mr. Plageanos."

Milos sighed, sliding slightly against his black satin sheets as he shifted. "Better now that you are here."

Taking out her stethoscope, Kady looked at him pointedly. "And before I was here?"

Milos spread his hands wide with a little half shrug. "Not so good."

Men didn't like to talk about health. Kady knew that like so many people, Milos had harbored the thought, the dream, that he was immortal. That whatever illnesses had been visited upon his forefathers wouldn't dare touch him. Finding out that he was wrong did not sit well with him.

She looked at the man, not with pity or sympathy, but with understanding. No one liked to think of their own mortality.

"I need more than that, Mr. Plageanos." Kady paused to look over her shoulder at both Byron and Ari. The latter lumbered to his feet. "I need you two to wait outside while I examine my patient."

Ari went out. After a moment's hesitation, Byron turned to do the same. "I'll be right back," he told his employer. "I want to talk to the driver about the car. It was making a weird noise when it turned left."

Milos nodded. "See why I keep him? Details. He is always thinking about details. A good man to have around." And then he smiled and winked at Byron as he walked past him. "Maybe this time she'll have her way with me," he chuckled.

Kady put the stethoscope around her neck. "I came to prevent a heart attack, Mr. Plageanos, not to give you one." Tickled, Milos began to laugh, so hard he started coughing. She was quick to place her hand on his chest, as if to steady him. "Easy, Mr. Plageanos, easy."

As the laughter died and the door to the bedroom was eased shut, Kady unbuttoned the top of Milos's silk pajamas and placed the stethoscope to his chest.

He yelped. "That's cold!" he cried as he shivered.

She pulled it back immediately. "Sorry." Kady blew on the silver surface, rubbing it against her palm to warm it up. After a beat she tried again. This time he didn't jerk back. "Better?"

He nodded, never taking his eyes off her face. "Better."

She frowned slightly. "Your heart's still jumping around." How long had that been going on? she wondered.

The exam was thorough but swift. Milos had even bought his own personal EKG machine so that he didn't have to go into her office to have his heart monitored. And during the exam, Kady asked a few pertinent questions in between dodging blatant invitations they both knew he would never act on and neither would she. Her questions encompassed his lifestyle, what he'd been eating lately, what he'd been doing. His diet remained relatively unchanged. His activity, however, had heightened.

She listened and watched his face as Milos told her about the other company, Skourous Shipping, the one that was breathing down his neck and had been for quite some time now. Alexander Skourous and his grandson, Nicholas, were trying to steal his customers any way they could, he told her, the veins in his neck thickening as he spoke.

The rivalry between Milos Plageanos and Alexander Skourous, whose families had both originated from the same small fishing village in the south of Greece, had been steadily heating up over the past twenty-five years. In the last five, it had gotten especially ugly. Matters were not helped by the fact that Milos's second wife had eloped with him a week before she was set to marry Alexander.

"This is not over the woman," Milos assured her. "For that, Alexander should have sent me a thank-you note because I saved him from a terrible shrew. But he is trying to steal my oldest customer from me. My very first one," he emphasized. "Theo is gone now, but his grandson…"

He waved his hand, unable to finish his sentence because the words he wanted to use to describe what he thought of his old friend's grandson weren't fit for her ears. In some ways, Milos was very much a courtly gentleman and she appreciated it.

Milos sat up, buttoning his pajama top as she put her stethoscope away. "I am a sentimental man—"

"Not to mention a superstitious one," Kady

pointed out, pausing to write something down on her prescription pad.

"Superstition is healthy." Leaning back against his pillows again, he eyed the pad suspiciously. "It tells us where our place is."

"I want you to stop thinking about the business so much and start thinking about you."

"I *am* the business and the business is me," he said with finality, then he nodded toward the pad. "What is that you are writing?"

"A prescription." She tore off the top page and held it out to him.

He made no effort to take it from her. "I have no time to go to the hospital."

"Good." Opening his hand, she placed the paper in it, then pushed his fingers closed again. "Because you're not going."

The pain had been real. And frightening. It was clear he didn't believe himself out of the woods yet. "I'm dying?"

She laughed warmly, placing her hand on top of his and patting it reassuringly. "You'll outlive me, Mr. Plageanos."

He frowned, shaking his head. "I have no wish to live in a world without beauty."

The man would be a player on his deathbed, she thought. Kady rolled her eyes. "I have to be getting back." She nodded at the paper in his hand. "Have one of your people fill that."

He looked at it, but without his glasses all he saw were wavy lines on a page. "What is this?"

She told him the name of the medication, then explained. "It's for your anxiety attack—the next time you have one."

An indignant expression came over his face. "I was not attacked by anxiety." Making a fist, he brought it in contact with his chest. "My heart attacked me."

She knew what the problem was. Men like Milos associated anxiety with weakness. They didn't understand that at times, the mind and body had wills of their own that had nothing to do with what a person might want or expect.

"Not this time. What you had was an anxiety attack—with a touch of heartburn." Lowering her voice, she leaned over his bed. "Stop eating all these rich Greek dishes, Mr. Plageanos. And cut down on the pastries." She indicated the plate of half-finished confection that was on his other nightstand.

"Stop eating baklava?" The instruction brought a look of mock distress to his face. "But eating baklava is like going to heaven."

"You'll be booking passage to there permanently if you're not careful." Closing her medical bag, she picked it up. "You have the constitution of a man half your age, but you have to take care of your-self—otherwise all this—" she waved around the huge room "—gets wasted."

He looked at the paper in his hand, his expression dubious. "Anxiety?"

"Anxiety," she affirmed.

Folding the paper again, he drew in his breath, resigned. "You can't tell anyone."

"No," she agreed, not knowing if he was ordering her or requesting it of her. In any event, she had her ethics. "I can't. I'm your doctor. This is just between you and me, remember? Now if you don't mind, I'd like to wash up before I leave." She glanced over her shoulder at the door. With Byron gone, she had no way of knowing which way to turn. "Where can I—?"

"No need to go anywhere, use mine." He gestured toward the sumptuous bathroom at the far end of the room. The door stood open, and from where she stood, Kady could just about make out the black onyx tiles. The man certainly did like black, she mused.

Nodding, she started across the room.

Chapter 2

The master bathroom was larger than her bedroom back at the apartment. As a matter of fact, Kady thought, taking a long look around, this bathroom looked larger than her living room. Not to mention that the gold sink and tub fixtures probably cost more than a year's rent.

She shook her head as she turned the handles and proceeded to wash her hands. What did a man need with a gold swan spouting out an arc of water into a black onyx tub? She dried her hands on towels that felt softer than whipped cream.

Moving over to the tub, Kady paused to look at it more closely. A huge stained-glass window directly behind it cast beams of blue and gold into the room. The tub itself was round and roomy enough for three wide-hipped people to sit comfortably without touching.

Opulence run amok, she couldn't help thinking.

It seemed like such a waste. The money that all this had cost would have been put to better use funding another clinic or helping to get people off the streets and on their feet again.

Kady straightened the towel she'd used and backed away. It was Milos's money, she told herself, and she had no right to impose her own set of values on him. The man should be free to enjoy it. Heaven knew he seemed to enjoy very little these days, focusing exclusively on his company and obsessing about it the way he did. It wasn't healthy. At his age, a man as well off as Milos should have no reason to stress himself out to the point of having an anxiety attack. He should be into the coasting part of his life.

And then she smiled. She sincerely doubted if she'd be willing to just coast at seventy. She'd still want to work, still want to make a difference. She supposed that was what kept the man going, a sense of purpose. Work, if you didn't hate it, was what kept you young. And Milos just told her that he considered the business his life and—

About to go back into the bedroom, her hand on the doorknob, Kady paused, cocking her head.

Trying to make out a sound. She could have sworn
she heard a series of popping noises coming from
somewhere within the bedroom. If she didn't know
better, she would have said they sounded like firecrackers.

Kady frowned slightly. All right, what was Milos
trying to pull now? She knew he thought himself
invincible, but she wanted him to spend the rest of
the day in bed. Anxiety attacks were not heart
attacks, but they could certainly feel that way to the
body, and after that kind of an ordeal, Milos's body
deserved to rest.

Now that she'd told Milos that the situation wasn't
actually dangerous, he was probably champing at the
bit to get back into the game of besting Skourous and
his company, making sure the other man had no opportunity to get the better of him.

She sighed, shaking her head.

With a reprimand on her tongue, all set for release, Kady opened the bathroom door.

And stopped dead.

There was someone else in the room. Someone
dressed all in black, right down to the gloves on his
hands and the shoes on his feet.

The collar of the turtleneck pullover was raised
up high, covering his mouth and his nose. Even his
eyes seemed to be coal black. The only thing of
vague color was the gun in his hand. Gray. The
gun's barrel appeared strangely disproportioned.

And then she recognized it for what it was. A silencer. The intruder had a silencer at the end of the gun barrel.

He'd come to kill someone.

He *had* killed someone, she realized in the next moment. That was what the noise had been. Bullets fired through a silencer.

Milos was lying in bed the way she'd left him, except that now there was a pool of blood on his wide chest. The sight of another figure, crumpled on the floor, registered less than a beat later.

Byron?

No, whoever it was was built smaller than the man who had accompanied her to the penthouse.

And then her heart felt as if it was constricting into a hot ball within her chest.

Ari.

Ari was lying there at the foot of Milos's bed. The other bodyguard must have rushed in when he heard the "pop" and had died trying to protect Milos.

Where was Byron? Was he lying somewhere, hurt? Dying? Dead? Kady felt her throat tightening more and more.

All these thoughts flew through her brain a beat before she pulled back into the bathroom, afraid that the killer would see her, too.

Her heart racing, Kady resisted the temptation to close the door again. Any unnecessary movement or sound might catch the killer's attention, make him come closer to investigate.

But she couldn't just stand here, frozen. Not knowing. What if he came after her?

With her heart racing faster than she thought humanly possible, Kady angled one of the three adjacent medicine cabinet mirrors to see what the killer was doing. To her surprise, he unscrewed the silencer from the gun barrel, tucking the former into his pocket and the latter into the back of the waistband of his slacks and then smoothed down his collar. As if appearance counted.

When he turned toward the door, she caught a clear glimpse of him, his image reversed in the mirror. Tall, his slight build appearing thinner because of the black clothing he wore, the killer looked young. Maybe twenty-eight, maybe less. He had a mop of curly black hair that looked as if a comb could get lost there.

She had no idea who he was. And then she saw his eyes. They weren't looking at her, but even at this distance, she'd never seen eyes so dead before.

She had to struggle to keep from shivering, from making a sound.

The killer paused at the door, listening. Kady held her breath. Had he heard her? She didn't think so, but she couldn't tell. Very carefully, she shrank back in the bathroom, making sure that her image wasn't thrown back at him in the mirrors.

In the recesses of the bathroom, she could no longer see what was happening. Her insides felt like jelly. She counted off seconds in her head, waiting. Mentally reciting a fragment of a prayer the sisters at St. Catherine's had taught her.

Finally the door opened and then closed again. As she eased back into range in the bathroom, her eyes were glued to the mirror. The outer door remained closed. It looked as if the shooter was gone.

Only then did she let out the breath she'd been holding. The next moment Kady shot out of the bathroom and rushed first to check the man on the floor. One look told her that Ari had been shot where he stood. She would have expected him to be disposed of the moment he'd entered the room. What was he doing clear across here, on the other side of Milos's bed?

Probably following the killer's orders, hoping to stay alive, she thought. Just like her.

Ari was dead. Had probably been dead even before he'd hit the floor. There was a single bullet hole in the center of his forehead.

She didn't remember crossing to the bed. The next thing she knew she was bending over Milos, searching for a pulse. Willing him to live. At first she couldn't find any evidence of a pulse, but then, squeezing her fingers hard over the man's thick wrist, she thought she detected the faintest hint of erratic rhythm.

He was alive.

She needed to keep him that way.

Her bag was still in the bathroom where she'd taken it, but she didn't want to leave Milos's side.

Her heart froze in midbeat as she saw his electric-blue eyes flutter open. Milos's lips moved, but she couldn't hear anything. Leaning in closer, she felt the faint brush of his breath against her cheek and thought she heard him say, "Skourous," but she couldn't have sworn to it.

"Don't talk," she ordered. "We'll get you to the hospital. You're going to be all right, Milos," she promised hoarsely. "You're going to be all right."

Kady wasn't even aware that she was crying, or that her tears were falling on the old man's face. She saw his lips move again, forming one word. "Liar."

And then his eyes fluttered shut.

Horror filled her. The next moment she'd gone on autopilot. She began applying CPR in a last-ditch effort to get Milos's heart beating again, however faintly. She wasn't about to let him die right in front of her.

Coming back from downstairs, Byron didn't think anything of it when he didn't see Ari standing guard outside Milos's bedroom. He'd just assumed that the examination was over and the man he shared bodyguard duties with had gone back into the room.

But when he knocked and heard Kady scream for him, his entire body immediately became alert. Throwing the doors open, he pulled out the weapon he wore holstered beneath his jacket.

A swift visual sweep of the room told him that there was no one else there. Only Ari on the floor, dead from the looks of it, and his employer in the bed, with the doctor frantically working over him.

Frantically trying to tug Milos away from the jaws of death.

"What the hell happened?" he demanded, crossing to her.

Her hair was falling into her face. Kady shook her head, trying to get it out of her eyes. She didn't look in his direction as the sound of his voice registered. She just kept going. Fighting.

"I don't know. Someone got in here. When I opened the bathroom door, he'd already shot both of them."

With amazing speed, Byron checked all the corners, making sure that there was no one else hiding in the recesses. He went back to her.

"Who?" he demanded.

"I don't know." Her voice cracked as she kept on pushing at the chest that made no movement on its own, kept blowing into a mouth that was already beginning to feel cool beneath hers.

Distancing himself, Byron processed the scene. Her efforts were futile. There was too much blood.

The bullet had been straight to Milos' chest. Straight to his heart, he guessed. The old man never stood a chance.

He cursed silently that he hadn't been here. That he'd been downstairs, talking to the mechanic Milos kept on the payroll to care for his twelve automobiles, instead of guarding Milos.

"He's dead, Doctor."

The low, calm voice seemed to rumble at her from some faraway place. She shook her head adamantly, never looking up, never stopping.

"No. No, he's not." She'd found a pulse. He'd tried to speak. She couldn't just let Milos slip away.

And then she felt strong, firm hands on either side of her shoulders, lifting her up, drawing her away from the bed. From the man she couldn't save.

Kady wanted to push the bodyguard away, wanted to go back and fight a fight she knew in her heart she'd already lost. But Byron was too strong for her. His grip was gentle but firm, holding her in place.

Suddenly, as if all the air had gone out of her, Kady felt weak, dizzy. The room began to spin. For a second it threatened to pull itself into darkness, leaving her on the outside to fend for herself. It was through sheer grit that she fought her way back from the blurred boundaries, fought back the nausea.

Trying to get a grip, Kady drew a deep breath into her lungs before she looked up at the man holding her. She saw concern in his eyes. Or maybe she just imagined it.

Either way, she felt like an idiot. She was made of sterner stuff than this. "Sorry. I don't usually fall apart like this."

"I don't see any pieces," he replied crisply. She felt fragile, like the scent of cherry blossoms. He hesitated backing off. "If I let you go, do you think you can stand?"

She raised her chin and tried to sound confident. Inside, the jelly had yet to solidify. "Yes."

He let her go by degrees, holding her a moment longer, then drawing his hands away slowly. All the while, he watched her face for any telltale signs that she would collapse or faint once he took his support away. There wasn't anything he could do for Milos, or Ari. But there was something he could do for her. He could keep her together.

Quickly, his eyes swept over her torso, checking. "Are you hurt?"

"No."

At least not physically, she thought. But mentally, she knew she was shell-shocked and would be for some time to come. It seemed strange to her that nothing like this had ever happened to her in the clinic where she volunteered. There she would have expected it. Yet here, in an exclusive neighborhood, she'd been a hair's breadth away from being killed.

Her eyes met his. Her lips felt dry as she spoke. "I don't think the killer saw me."

"Was there only one?" he wanted to know.

She couldn't answer that with certainty. All she could tell Byron was what she knew. "There might have been more, but I only saw one man."

Kady looked back over her shoulder at the man who'd flirted with her only ten minutes ago. He'd been so vibrant, so full of life then. And now…

This shouldn't have happened.

She looked back at Byron again. "What kind of security system does this penthouse have?" she demanded angrily. Shouldn't something have gone off when the killer got in? When he escaped?

"One that was obviously bypassed." Unlike hers, Byron's voice was stoic.

Releasing her, he walked over to the intercom located on the wall beside Milos's bed. There was an intercom in every room of the penthouse. Pressing the button down, Byron said, "This is Byron. I want everyone up here outside Mr. Plageanos's bedroom. Now."

Was he planning on interrogating everyone on the staff? That wasn't how things were done. With a heavy heart, Kady moved back to the bed. To the man she'd come to regard with affection.

I'm sorry I couldn't save you.

Looking up, she saw Byron watching her. Kady braced her shoulders. "You have to call the police."

He looked at her for a long moment before answering. Was he annoyed because she'd said that? Did he think she was trying to tell him what to do?

"I know procedure."

The way he said it made her think he'd been through this before. And made her realize that she really knew nothing about this man she'd shared less than a handful of car rides with.

"You're a cop?"

"Was," he corrected.

Like her sisters, she possessed more than her share of curiosity. Even in the face of tragedy, she needed to know things.

"What happened?" she heard herself asking.

Byron didn't answer. Instead, he shook his head. "Too much to talk about now."

Kady wasn't completely certain she could assimilate anything he told her now anyway. So she nodded, letting the matter drop. Digging into her pocket, Kady pulled out her cell phone and then flipped it open.

Byron looked at her sharply. "Who are you calling?"

God, but she felt drained. Drained and useless and angry. She felt as if she was going in all directions at once. His tone irritated her more than it should have.

"My brother-in-law. He *is* a cop," she told him. "Homicide. Tony Santini."

The information came in small, square sound bites, dribbling from her lips. Kady clung to the numbness, knowing that once it was gone, what would come in its wake would be overwhelming and devastating.

Crossing back to her, Byron placed his hand over her cell phone and closed it, leaving it in the palm of her hand. Kady looked at him, confused. "We have to call the police," she insisted.

"And I will. If your brother-in-law is called in to investigate, there might be questions later on."

She stared at him. "Questions?"

"Mr. Plageanos was a powerful man. Powerful men have enemies—enemies with money who can get to people."

Her eyes widened and she drew herself up. "Are you saying—"

He shook his head. "I'm not, but someone else might. You were the last person to see him alive. Having your brother-in-law here isn't the wisest move."

"Right."

She wasn't thinking straight, Kady acknowledged. She just wanted someone to make it right. She wanted someone to catch the killer and avenge Milos and Ari. She wanted the man she'd seen put in prison. Now, before he could do any more harm.

With a sigh Kady dragged a hand through her hair. "You're right," she repeated.

She stiffened as she heard a sound in the hall, then realized it was too loud to be the killer. It was the sound of approaching feet. The people Byron had just summoned were here. Right outside the threshold to Milos's bedroom. Exclamations of distress, of horror, were heard as the scene was suddenly viewed by them. One of the maids fainted. The chauffeur pushed through the doorway as questions flew right and left.

Byron stopped everyone at the threshold, physically blocking their access into the room. Quickly his eyes swept over the group. Kady had a feeling he was trolling for a killer.

Was it one of the staff? A chill passed over her as she looked from face to face. But he wasn't there. The man who'd been in the room only a few minutes ago wasn't here.

"It's a crime scene," he told the staff in a voice devoid of emotion. "I called you up here because I wanted you to know that someone just killed Mr. Plageanos." And because, he added silently, he wanted to see their reactions.

"How?"

"Who?"

Surprise and shock mingled with half sentences; expressions of outrage and curses blended into one another. Byron gave it a few minutes, letting grief and disbelief run their initial course before he held up his hand for silence.

"That's what we're going to find out," he promised without fanfare. "Right now I'd say that someone inside let the killer in." He looked over the sea of faces slowly, seeming to focus on each individually. He was looking for an accomplice. Again, there was no emotion as he said, "Whoever it is will be made to pay so they'd better get their affairs in order."

Like a second tidal wave, more questions and protests arose, drowning each other out. It was all just dissonance to her.

Kady moved back toward the bathroom, unaware that she was being watched. Once inside, at the sink, she struggled to keep the tears back. The control she was trying to grasp continued to elude her.

She looked down at her hands covered in Milos's blood. Very slowly, she turned on the faucets and began to wash her hands. Rivulets of pink snaked their way to the drain and beyond. She tried to make her mind a blank until she could deal with it all.

But thoughts insisted on crowding in.

Had she not withdrawn into the bathroom just when she had, she could very well be lying in a pool of blood beside Ari and Milos.

Sensing she wasn't alone, Kady looked up into the mirror and saw Byron standing behind her in the doorway. Their eyes met.

"I called the police," he told her quietly. "You're going to have to give a statement."

Gripping the faucets, she turned them off simultaneously. She continued holding them for a moment, as if they were all that was keeping her from sinking to the floor. "I know."

"After that," he said, sounding as if he was reciting some preauthorized schedule, "I'll have someone drive you home."

She turned around to face Byron. "How can you be so calm?" she demanded.

His face was completely unreadable. "Practice."

Chapter 3

Detective Larry Wilkins of the New York Police Department, Homicide Division, was born worn around the edges, rumpled and suspicious. He operated each of his investigations from the standpoint that everyone was guilty until proven otherwise. At least ten pounds overweight and wearing clothes that hadn't seen a hanger in over a decade, he had a habit of invading people's personal space when he spoke to them. He thought of it as a useful technique during an investigation.

Right now, as he questioned her, Kady could all but taste the pizza he'd had for dinner last night. It was apparent to her that the detective was immersed in a love affair with extra garlic. It took all her strength not to turn her head away.

Detective Wilkins looked at her as if he'd already made up his mind that she had either killed Milos Plageanos herself, or masterminded the murder.

Holding on to a much-used notebook, Wilkins looked at her with small brown eyes that could have cut holes through a steel plate.

"And you were in the bathroom the entire time the murders went down?"

She'd already told him that. Twice. Wilkins made it sound as if she'd spent an eternity in the room when it had merely felt that way. In total, she'd been there maybe five minutes, maybe less.

It didn't take long to end a man's life, Kady thought.

Wilkins had her isolated in one corner of Milos's bedroom. She tried desperately to block out the sounds of the forensic team as they went about their business, gathering evidence that attested to the last moments of the billionaire's life.

"Yes," she answered again, then couldn't help adding, "But I don't think it took too long to shoot two people."

A smirk raised the corners of Wilkins's mouth. It reminded her of a hyena waiting for lunch. "Timed it, did you?" He took a step in, cutting the space between them. "During the actual occurrence or the dry run?"

"Dry run?" she echoed, stunned. He actually

thought she had something to do with it. How dare he? "I don't know what you're talking about."

The smirk deepened. "Sure you do. You and your accomplice probably did a dry run to see how long it would actually take to walk in and shoot the old guy and his bodyguard."

She stared at him. The man was insane. Completely, utterly insane. "What possible reason would I have to kill Mr. Plageanos?"

Heavyset shoulders rose and fell beneath a houndstooth jacket that looked slept in. "Dunno yet. But I'll find out."

Anger came streaking in on a lightning bolt, fueled by exhaustion and powered by exasperation. Her eyes blazed as she looked at this would-be Colombo. He was forgetting one very salient point. "And did I plan his anxiety attack, too?"

It was evident that Wilkins had expected her to be intimidated, cowed, not furious. He glared at his notes. "Thought the old guy had a heart attack."

He would have gotten that information from someone else, she thought. Kady took offense at the cavalier way he dismissed the late shipping magnate.

"*Mr. Plageanos* had an anxiety attack, not a heart attack," she corrected tersely. "And the reason he had the attack was because he was a micromanager who took everything to heart." She drew herself up to her full five-four stature, wishing it wasn't against the law to punch out a police detective. "I had no way of knowing that I was even going to *be* here today. How the hell could I have planned this?" she demanded.

"You planned for the eventuality," Wilkins countered, but it was obvious that he was losing steam. Some part of him was being won over by the idea that her only crime was being in the wrong place at the wrong time. Still, he wasn't about to give up all at once. "Maybe disarmed the security system so that your man could come in."

"And maybe I smuggled 'my man' in my medicine bag," she retorted sarcastically. Struggling, she regained control of her temper. "Look, Detective, I'm a cardiologist, not an electronics technician. The only thing I was doing here today was responding to Mr. Plageanos's request for medical attention." Her voice began to rise by increments. "Now why don't you stop making ridiculous accusations and get me together with a sketch artist so I can describe the man who killed Mr. Plageanos and Ari."

For a moment the look on Wilkins's face was triumphant, as if he thought he had her. "You saw the guy's face. This guy you didn't know." Half a foot taller than Kady, he leaned in, bringing his face close to hers for emphasis. "I thought you said you were in the bathroom."

She was sorely tempted to dig into her purse and hand the man breath mints. "I was," she said in between clenched teeth.

"Then how did you see his face?"

Instead of answering, Kady let out an angry sigh and turned on her heel.

Stunned, Wilkins called after her. "Hey, we're not through here. Where the hell do you think you're going?" he demanded. When she didn't turn around, he shoved the notebook into his back pocket and hurried after her.

"To show you," Kady tossed over her shoulder. Walking into the bathroom, she deliberately left the door wide open, the way it had been before. She opened the medicine cabinet and angled the mirrored door so that it reflected the interior of the bedroom. "I saw him like this."

Wilkins craned his neck, coming over to her side of the room. From where he stood, Milos's bed was clearly visible. The detective chewed on the inside of his check as he continued to glare at the mirrors. Finally he exhaled rather loudly.

"Smart," he allowed grudgingly.

It was the first decent thing she'd heard the man say since he'd pounced on her. Vindicated, Kady chose not to comment—just in case it was another verbal trap. To her way of thinking, her action hadn't been smart so much as desperate.

Wilkins began flipping through the notes he'd jotted down during her recounting of the events. Kady couldn't help wondering just how much he'd annotated. For the first time in her life, she understood what the term *railroaded* meant.

Finally Wilkins flipped the cover closed, returned the pad to his back pocket and nodded. "Okay," he said. "I'll have someone take you in to the station. You can work with a sketch artist."

"I'll take her," Byron volunteered quietly.

The sound of his voice coming up behind her surprised Kady. She thought he was downstairs with the other detective. The bodyguard seemed to materialize out of nowhere.

Had he been there all the time, listening?

Wilkins had blotted out everything with his close proximity, keeping her from being aware of anything else but him. She knew the detective had meant for it to be that way.

Byron had been the first to be questioned, but he had caught Wilkins's partner instead of Wilkins. Luck of the draw, she supposed.

She saw Wilkins look at Byron for a long moment, then the older man passed a hand over his all but bald pate and snarled, "Okay. You know the way."

Byron met Wilkins's scrutiny without flinching. "Yeah, I know the way."

"Why do you know the way?" Kady asked the bodyguard several minutes later as they left the penthouse.

Just before they left the building, they passed one of the maids. The young woman, not more than twenty-two, was standing off to the side, sobbing.

Kady fought the urge to stop and comfort her. But her morning was quickly disappearing and she still had a practice waiting for her. Mercifully, Mondays she went to the office in the afternoon.

Byron made no answer. He led her to a well-cared-for Nissan Z. She knew little about cars, but decided it had to be old since the insignia on the back said Datsun instead of Nissan. He opened the passenger door for her.

Getting in, she looked at Byron. "Or am I not supposed to ask?"

Byron got in on his side and turned the ignition on. The car hummed to life. "You can ask."

He picked his way through the maze of police cars and the coroner's van crowding the exit of the underground parking structure. His voice had trailed off even before they hit the street.

"But will you answer?" she probed. And then she made an attempt to fill in the blank herself. "Did you work out of that precinct?" He looked at her sharply just before he made a turn. "You said you were a cop once," she reminded him.

He nodded. He'd forgotten he told her. Milos's murder had thrown everything else into the background. He hadn't deserved to have been cut down that way. If he'd had to die in his bed, it should have been after enjoying himself with a lusty, willing partner. He should have died with a smile on his face, not staring into a gun barrel.

Kady was still waiting for an answer. With a shrug, he gave her one. "I was based in Brooklyn."

"And they had an exchange program with the detectives in Manhattan?"

It was an absurd thing to say and she knew it, but she was trying to get him to talk, create some distraction from the thoughts of what she'd just left behind and what she'd been a witness to. Besides, she knew nothing about this stoic man beside her. She wanted a few blanks filled in.

He laughed shortly at the display of tenacity. "There was an attempted robbery at the penthouse about six months ago." He had caught the thief before the man could get away, but he left that part unspoken. "I took Mr. Plageanos in to file a report."

The details didn't quite jibe but she couldn't think of a reason why Byron would lie to her. Something was missing. "And Wilkins was working the Robbery Division at the time?"

"Our paths crossed."

The answer told her nothing except that he wasn't willing to talk about it. Frustrated, Kady blew out a breath. It was like trying to get into a conversation with the sphinx.

"Okay, you pick the topic."

He spared her a glance as he stepped on the gas, making it through the amber light before it turned red. The streets were swollen with cars. "What?"

"Well, you obviously don't want to answer any

questions and I'm not in the mood to sit here beside you in silence until we get to the police station, so talk about anything you want to. Just talk," Kady added with emphasis.

He made a right at the end of the next block. Kady couldn't tell if he was amused, or if it was just the angle of his profile that made him look as if his lips were curving.

"It might have escaped you," he finally said, "but I don't talk much."

"No, it hasn't escaped me." It wouldn't have escaped her even if she'd been a single-cell amoeba. "But I thought in light of everything, today might be a good day to start."

He didn't follow her logic, but then, she was a woman and he found that he'd never been able to tune in to the way they thought, a by-product of being raised by just his father. "Why?"

Ordinarily she didn't like to showcase a weakness. She prided herself on being strong. But today someone had thrown out the rule book.

"Because I don't want to cry, and right now I'm about this far away from it." Kady held her thumb and forefinger an inch apart almost directly in front of him.

He moved her hand aside so that he could see the road more clearly. "Didn't sound like you were going to cry when Wilkins was questioning you." Again, that odd little half smile took possession of his mouth. "I thought I might be called in to restrain you."

He *was* amused, she thought. "You heard?"

He inclined his head in an abbreviated nod. "Got a temper on you," he observed, then glanced at her as they came to a red light. "Wouldn't think it to look at you."

As far as she was concerned, she had good reason to be angry. "Wilkins was accusing me of being involved in Mr. Plageanos's murder."

"Wilkins accuses everyone. It's what he does. Or did," he added. The last part was under his breath. "It levels the playing field for him."

She'd thought that some sort of recognition had passed between the two men. "Then you do know him."

He wouldn't exactly say that. He doubted that anyone really knew Wilkins. He knew that no one really knew him. He didn't let people in. Not anymore. "I told you, our paths have crossed."

Kady read between the lines. "Not over the burglary," she surmised.

Annoyed, Byron blew out a breath. The woman just didn't back off. He looked at her. "You're like a junkyard dog, you know that?"

"No," she contradicted with a smile, denying the comparison. "I'm Polish."

Eyebrows as dark as night drew together over the bridge of his nose. "What the hell does that have to do with it?"

She'd learned a long time ago that beyond demeaning ethnic jokes, most people have a very limited knowledge of anything Polish. She set about educating him. "Polish women are known for their stubbornness."

He didn't know about Polish women being stubborn, but she damn well was. "I didn't know."

"Now you do." She paused, waiting. Byron made no effort to continue. Biting back a sigh, she prodded him again. "You were about to tell me about crossing paths with Wilkins."

For a moment Byron debated telling her to back off, then decided that it didn't matter anymore. Nothing mattered anymore. Not since Bobby died. "Wilkins used to be with IAB."

"The Internal Affairs Bureau?" she cut in. Now that she thought of it, the man was perfect for it. He was relentless and intimidating and, she had no doubt, probably ruthless as well, given half a chance. He'd probably loved his job.

Byron looked at her, mildly impressed. "You know about IAB?"

"Sure." And for the first time since she'd gone in to wash her hands after examining Milos, she grinned. "I watch TV like everyone else." But because the subject was serious, she sobered again before asking, "What was it that Wilkins investigated?"

The moment the question was out of her mouth, she knew.

"You?" She saw his jaw harden. She didn't think

of herself as the world's best judge of character, but she was pretty high up there, she reasoned. IAB investigated cops who were crooked. Her gut told her that Byron was as honest as they came. "Why?"

"Every time a detective discharges his weapon, there's an investigation." He stared straight ahead, his hands tightening on the steering wheel. He was beginning to regret his offer to bring her down here.

"And did you? Kill someone?" she prompted when silence was the only answer that greeted her.

"Yeah." He slanted a look in her direction. "You don't remember me, do you?"

By the way Byron asked the question, she knew he wasn't referring to anything recent, nor was he referring to the time he'd brought his employer into the E.R. But instinct told her it had to have had something to do with the E.R. That would explain why, the first time she recalled meeting him, she'd had this nagging feeling that she'd seen him before. At the time she'd chalked it up to someone looking like him. So many faces came and went in the E.R., it was hard to remember them all.

"Not specifically," she admitted. "Although I've had this feeling that I've seen you before you walked into the E.R. with Mr. Plageanos."

He nodded, hardly hearing. "I came in the ambulance with this rookie cop." His voice was completely dead, as if he was reading lines from a teleprompter. "He was off duty and he'd walked into this mom and pop deli to pick up some provolone for his brother."

This was hard for him, Kady thought, watching as each word labored its way past his lips. She kept her peace, waiting for him to go on.

"There was a robbery going on. The rookie tried to stop it."

His voice died away. He couldn't just leave her dangling here. "How did you figure into it?" she finally asked quietly.

He took his time replying. She could have sworn that he was physically erecting a wall around himself. A wall between him and the pain the words caused.

"I was in the car, waiting."

She made the natural assumption. "You were the brother?"

He nodded so slowly she thought his head hadn't moved. "I was the brother." And then his voice hardened. "I should have been the one who went in, not him, but there was a news bulletin on the radio and I wanted to hear the end of it. So Bobby hopped out of the car and went into the deli. The next thing I knew, there were gunshots and then this tall, skinny guy, still holding a piece, came running out. It was as if I saw the whole thing that had happened inside in slow motion. I yelled out that I was a cop, told the guy to stop. When he didn't, I shot him." He didn't add that he'd looked into the store and saw Bobby on the ground in a pool of his own blood, or that the robber had turned his weapon on him and was about to fire when he killed him.

"It was a clean shoot."

She said it with such confidence, he had to look at her. He would have said she was pandering, but there was nothing to gain. So he shrugged it off. "Wilkins didn't see it that way."

Wilkins, she decided, was a man that people could easily hate. "They brought you up on charges?" she asked incredulously.

"No, I was cleared." But it had been close for a while. IAB had everyone afraid of coming forward. It was as if, to prove everyone was vigilant, a scapegoat had to be sacrificed. "And then I quit."

If there were no charges, he should have remained to work toward his pension. To leave seemed foolish. "But why?"

He'd thought of the police force as his family. The family—except for Bobby—that he had never actually had. When Bobby died, and everyone on the force backed away while the investigation was ongoing, he felt as if he'd lost everything. His marriage, such as it was, fell apart. So, he'd shut down and backed away himself.

"Didn't seem to be any purpose to staying on a force that turns against you just when you need support." And then his own words played themselves back to him. His expression hardened as he turned to her. He looked formidable. "Why are you asking all these questions?"

"Because I want to know," she replied simply.

That still didn't tell him anything. "Why? We're strangers."

Her answer surprised him. "Only because you want it that way." When he looked at her quizzically, she added, "Me, I make friends with everyone."

She was making assumptions. "Maybe I don't want any friends."

"Everyone wants friends," Kady countered quietly. "You just might not know it."

"Same thing," he insisted.

"No," she replied, her voice as firm as her belief, "it's not."

"We're here," he told her, pulling up into the parking lot.

And none too soon, he added silently.

Chapter 4

It was only after Kady had gotten together with the sketch artist, bringing to life the man she'd seen murder two innocent people, that she remembered. Remembered that the rookie policeman that she'd worked over in the E.R. that night Byron had re-created for her had died shortly after he'd been brought in. Died despite all her best efforts to save him. The damage had been too extensive.

Numbed, she looked around to see if she could glimpse Byron, but he was nowhere to be seen. Kady sighed inwardly. She'd been so involved in trying to secure bits and pieces of information from Byron, she'd missed the elephant in the living room.

"Something doesn't look right to you?" the technician asked, ready to hit another set of keys.

"No." She forced herself to focus on the image that was coming together on the screen. This needed to be out of the way first. "You're getting it."

"Good, now about his hair…"

As soon as the sketch artist completed the composite, Byron materialized at her elbow, almost as if he'd been standing behind some invisible curtain. One moment he wasn't there, the next, he was. It took everything she had not to jump. But inside, she could feel her adrenaline launch into high gear.

"How do you do that?" she wanted to know, turning to face Byron. "How do you suddenly just appear out of nowhere like that?"

The slightest hint of a smile whispered along his lips. She couldn't decide if he was patronizing her. "I don't. You just didn't notice me because you were distracted."

"I'd have to be dead not to notice you," she told him matter-of-factly.

Kady wasn't flirting with him, although God knew she'd done more than her share in med school, partying to shake off the stress of having to study all but nonstop for days on end. What she'd said had been a simple observation. She'd come to realize that Byron didn't say much verbally, but his presence certainly did. He had a commanding aura about him that turned all eyes in his direction. He was what her younger sister, Tania, would have referred to as drop-dead gorgeous.

Noting the way he handled himself, and because he'd once been a cop, Kady couldn't help wondering just how many people had dropped dead because of him.

There was an air of danger about Byron, and yet, for some reason, he made her feel safe.

Byron pretended that he hadn't heard her comment. Instead he asked, "Ready to go?" directing the question more to the man sitting at the computer than to her.

The computer technician nodded, then pushed up the glasses that had slid down his nose. "We're finished. Unless there's something else?" he added, looking at Kady.

"No, that's him," Kady said, taking one last look. "That's the man I saw leaving Mr. Plageanos's bedroom."

"Then she's all yours," the tech told Byron.

After thanking the technician, she rose and hurried after Byron, already headed for the door. Catching up, she pressed her lips together. She had no idea how to start. Full speed ahead was ordinarily her style, but it didn't seem to quite fit here. Part of her just wanted to let it go.

Still, she didn't want Byron to think that she was crass or insensitive. She wanted him to know that although she did deal with death on occasion, it wasn't just something she shrugged off without a backward glance. His brother had lost too much blood by the time she'd gotten to him. It wasn't a matter of her being in above her head, or not having enough expertise to save him. The man had been beyond anyone's ability to save. He'd needed a miracle and the hospital and she were fresh out of miracles that night.

That didn't make it any less of a loss. Not to her. Not to Byron.

Lost in thought, she'd managed to fall a little behind. "I'm sorry about your brother," she said to his back.

Leading the way out of the precinct to his vehicle, Byron looked over his shoulder at her. "What?"

"Your brother. Bobby." She'd remembered his name the moment the circumstances had come back to her. Almost skipping to cut the distance, she caught up to Byron, then continued to take long strides to match his pace. "He died that night. I'm sorry I couldn't save him."

He'd spent some time hating her, hating the hospital, the ambulance drivers, everyone. And then he'd turned that hate on himself. It never got him anywhere, but that was just the way things were. He was over it, mostly. He just hadn't for-given himself yet.

Byron pulled open the passenger door for her, then rounded the hood and got in on his side. She'd already buckled her belt by the time he got in.

"Wasn't your fault." The words were short, staccato, as if they were being fired out rapidly. "It was mine."

The wealth of guilt she heard in his voice was staggering. Had he been carrying that around all this time? It was a miracle that he hadn't self-destructed.

Byron pulled out of the lot, his profile rigid. A lesser woman would have backed away. But she had started this; she was going to see it through.

"You had no way of knowing what would happen to him," she said gently.

Knowing or not, that didn't change what he should have done. "I should have gone in and gotten my own damn cheese."

Her heart went out to him. He couldn't continue to carry this burden, couldn't continue beating himself up about it. "Things happen for a reason. Maybe you were supposed to stay alive."

He looked at her sharply. She would have drawn back if she hadn't been belted in. "And Bobby wasn't?"

That wasn't what she'd meant. Kady sighed, shaking her head. "You're a hard man to cheer up, Byron."

"There's a solution for that," he replied crisply. "Don't try."

Too late, she thought. It was obvious that Byron wanted her to stop talking, to slip into silence and pretend that nothing had been said. She was willing to drop the subject of his brother, but not to spend the rest of this trip in silence. What she'd witnessed was still too much with her, too raw. For now, she needed to be distracted and he was her only resource.

"What's your name?" she asked suddenly.

Caught off guard, Byron looked at her as if she'd lapsed into baby talk. "Did that gunman hit you in the head?"

"No, he never even saw me," she reminded him, incredibly grateful for that.

He frowned to himself as he went down a one-way street four miles over the posted speed limit. "Then why are you asking me what my name is? You know what it is. It's Byron."

She shifted in her seat, the belt digging into her hip as she turned to look at him. "Yes, I know, but is Byron your first name? Your last? Is it some nickname they pinned to you in elementary school?"

Maybe that getting-hit-in-the-head theory wasn't as far-fetched as it sounded. The woman was babbling, he thought. "What kind of nickname is Byron?"

She shrugged. It was possible. "Maybe your mother liked the romantic poets and saw a little of Lord Byron in you." Because, she added silently, if

Byron had been taller and believed in working out, she would have said that the man beside her was a dead ringer for the tragic poet.

"Never knew my mother," Byron answered curtly, hoping this would be the end of it. "She died after Bobby was born."

It seemed as if she couldn't win for losing. She hadn't meant to open any more old wounds. "Oh, I'm sorry."

Byron made no comment. Instead he continued to stare straight ahead at the road, his hands wrapped around the wheel.

Finally, after several minutes had passed, he shrugged. "It happens."

More often than he probably realized, she thought. That didn't take the sting away. "But it's still rough, growing up without a parent."

He slanted a look at her. Was she about to build on some common thread? "You?"

She felt almost guilty at having had the kind of childhood she'd had. Loving parents and sisters who would have done anything for her, would always be there for her if she needed them.

"No," she replied quietly. "Both of mine are still alive."

And probably doted on her, Byron guessed. She had that look about her. Hardest thing she probably had to deal with is finding a pair of shoes that went with the outfit she'd chosen.

"Then how would you know?" It almost sounded like an accusation.

The smile on her lips unsettled him. It was completely disarming. "I have a vivid imagination."

Byron laughed shortly. "I can believe that."

"So?" she asked, her tone light again as she attempted to get back to her original question.

Byron's eyebrows drew together, knotting in totally confusion as he glanced at her before switching lanes. "'So' what?"

Kady sighed. The man could bob and weave with the best of them. She wondered if he'd been a handful, growing up. And if he'd missed his mother, or at least the idea of a mother. Her heart ached a little, knowing how she would have felt without hers. Completely lost.

"Is Byron your first or last name?" she pressed.

It really was like dealing with a junkyard dog. "First," he ground out grudgingly.

Talk about baby steps. The man was not willing to meet her halfway, or even a quarter of the way. "Do you have a last name?" she finally asked when he volunteered nothing beyond the single word.

"Yeah."

Okay, he was doing this on purpose, she decided. "And is it a government secret?"

His voice was mild. If he didn't know better, he would have said he was even enjoying himself. "Not that I know of."

Byron paused, playing the moment out for his own amusement. He had no idea why the doctor's questioning amused more than annoyed him. Maybe it was because this pint-size doctor stood out from the rest of all the people he'd encountered since he'd come to work for the late shipping magnate. In a sea of interchangeable people, she was unique, like the color red in a box of beige crayons.

He could feel her looking at him. Waiting. He counted to ten, then said, "It's Kennedy."

"Kennedy," she repeated. With all his secrecy, she would have thought it was something akin to Rumpelstiltskin. She smiled at him. "Now, was that so hard?"

He merely shook his head. "You missed your calling, Doc. You should have gone into interrogation."

"Not interested." She dismissed the idea. "I like fixing people too much."

"If you say so."

Lapsing into silence, he continued driving. He seemed comfortable with the silence, or maybe comfortable with blocking her out. When she leaned over to switch the radio on, he said, "It's broken."

"Why don't you fix it?"

He shrugged. "Don't need it."

Why didn't that surprise her? She leaned back in

her seat again. There was only so much silence she could take. "So," she turned to look at his profile, "what are you going to do now?"

"Drop you off and then go back to the penthouse."

. She wondered if Milos had made provisions for his people. "I mean after that." She was willing to bet Byron knew she meant in the big-picture sense. "You're out of work."

He glanced at her for a split second. "Thanks for pointing that out."

She could feel herself bristling. Her father, Josef, was a retired NY policeman and he now worked at a security firm run by his ex-partner. She was about to ask Byron if he was interested in getting a job at the firm, but his manner made her hold back the question. "Do you answer everything with sarcasm?"

The car ahead of him braked suddenly, and he jammed on the brakes to avoid a collision. "Pretty much."

Kady ignored the near accident, focusing instead on Byron. "Why are you trying to keep everyone at bay?"

He hated anyone digging into his life. He had no need for labels, for trying to find reasons behind actions. He was what he was and made no apologies. "Cardiologist, interrogator, psychiatrist—how many hats are you planning on wearing, Doc?"

He was still pushing her away. But the harder he pushed, the more steadfast she was determined to remain. "Human beings are made up of a lot of parts, Byron. They're not just one-dimensional. I was just being—"

"Nosy?" he supplied.

"Concerned."

"Concerned?" he mocked. "Why? Until ten miles ago, you didn't even know my last name."

"But now I do," she pointed out. Before he could say anything, she added, "Maybe I'm concerned because I feel you need someone to be concerned about you."

She saw annoyance flare in his eyes. What had she said that was so wrong? "I'm not some stray dog you need to take in."

His tone warned her to back off. But she had never been one to run when she sensed someone in pain. There was a great deal of hurt beneath that gruff exterior of his. She could see it in his deep blue eyes, could hear it in his voice, even though she knew that Byron probably thought he'd hidden all the telltale signs well.

She smiled and said, "Nothing stray about you, Byron."

He made it through a yellow light, pulling up to the green awning that stood before the glass double doors. "We're here," he pointed out, nodding toward the apartment building.

She'd been too engrossed in trying to resurrect his soul to realize where they were. She looked to her right.

"So we are."

She glanced down at her blouse. There was still blood on it. Not exactly something to inspire confidence in her patients, she mused.

"Thanks," she murmured, expecting him to all but eject her from the vehicle.

When she began to get out and he put his hand on her arm, stopping her, she was thoroughly confused.

"You'll be all right?"

She tried to read between the lines, to find the hidden message. Was he actually expressing concern about her? No, it had to be something else.

"Going upstairs by myself?" she guessed, uncertain what he was asking. "Sure."

"No." He looked impatient. "I'm talking about what happened earlier. Are you going to be all right? Do you want me to come up with you?"

The smile came slowly, moving along her lips, slipping into her eyes. He was worried about her. Just when she'd decided that he was beyond reaching, he did something nice like this.

"I'll be all right," she assured him. "Thanks for asking."

Her gratitude made him uncomfortable. Any mention of his having done something nice made him feel uncomfortable. The moment the doctor was out of the car, he stepped on the gas and pulled away. Glad to be getting away.

As he melded into the clogged passage of mid-morning traffic, Byron glanced in his rearview mirror. The woman was still standing on the sidewalk, watching him drive down the block. He forced himself to look away before he got into an accident.

The moment she turned away and entered the building, her legs felt like lead.

Passing one of the tenants in the foyer, Kady was aware that the older woman was giving her a very scrutinizing look. Ordinarily, Kady would stop to say something, to explain why she looked like this. But right at this moment, she suddenly felt too tired to explain. Too tired to do anything but hope-fully get herself up to her apartment.

It occurred to her as she walked into the elevator that she had less than two hours before she was due at the hospital. Visions of falling into bed and curling up for half an eternity sorely tempted her. Her sense of responsibility arm-wrestled with her desire for sleep. Responsibility barely won.

Getting off the elevator, Kady spent the trip to her door searching for her keys. She managed to drop them not once but twice. The second time, just as she started to insert the tip of her key into the lock, they fell to the newly scrubbed tile hallway with a clang that echoed in her ears. She had more than a dozen keys on her keychain, and the right one always seemed to go into hiding the second she needed it. As she stooped down to pick them up and try again, the door to the apartment flew open.

"My God, where have you been?" Natalya demanded. She dropped down to her knees to be on her younger sister's level. "I was going out of my mind when they called from Patience Memorial, looking for you."

"Looking for me?" She wasn't due until this afternoon. Why were they calling Natalya? Oh God, she hoped they didn't call her parents' house. Mama would be out organizing a search party within five minutes of the call.

"One of your patients was trying to reach you and couldn't get through, so they called the E.R." Natalya tried to look stern. She'd had a pretty bad scare. "You didn't leave a note, you didn't—" And then her eyes widened as she looked at her sister, really looked at her. "Kady, there's blood on your clothes," she cried, stopping in midbreath. She grabbed her sister by the arms and rose up with her. "Kady, what happened?" She ran her hands up and down Kady's arms, then her sides, concerned. Looking for wounds. "Are you all right? You look like hell."

"Was that supposed to make me feel better?" she quipped. Kady dragged her hand through her hair. "Just had an extended night, that's all."

"And blood was involved?" Natalya's hands tightened on her sister's shoulders. "All right, spill it. Where were you and whose blood is that?"

Kady sighed. "Can I sit down?"

Realizing that she sounded like the military police, Natalya backed off. She brought Kady over to the sofa. "Sorry, sure." She paused, peering at Kady's face. "Do you want something to drink?"

"Is it too early for scotch?"

Natalya looked at her uncertainly. "Was it that bad?"

"Just kidding," Kady murmured.

But only partially, Kady thought. She could have used something stronger than water to see her through. But she couldn't afford the luxury of indulging herself. Or of calling in to have someone take over her shift. She had patients who were depending on her.

And right now, she thought, turning to look at Natalya, she had a sister who was waiting to grill her. She suddenly realized how Byron must have felt. Mentally she apologized to him.

Chapter 5

"Oh my God, you could have been killed!"

The words rushed out of Natalya's mouth the moment Kady finished. It was obvious to her that Kady had tried to give her a short, no-frills narrative of what had happened at the shipping magnate's apartment, but just the bare-bones details were enough to send Natalya's mind racing to other possible scenarios.

Natalya looked more shaken up than she was. "But I wasn't," Kady pointed out.

"But you could have been," Natalya insisted. There was horror in her eyes as she pushed away the thought that was too terrible to contemplate. Sitting beside Kady on the sofa, Natalya put her arms around her sister and held her tight for a moment. "I'm sorry you had to go through that," she said softly.

Kady knew she meant it. For a moment, feeling suddenly drained, she allowed herself the luxury of absorbing the comfort her sister was offering. For that moment everything inside her felt as if it was on the verge of collapsing.

"Not exactly something I'd recommend for a morning's diversion," Kady agreed with a dry laugh. And then, disengaging herself from her sister, she rose from the sofa.

Natalya was on her feet, too, searching for something to do to make her sister feel better, to balance out the ordeal Kady had just gone through. "Want me to draw you a hot bath?"

It sounded wonderful, but if she indulged, she doubted she'd ever leave the bathtub. Kady shook her head. "Don't have time for one. I've got to be at the hospital at one."

Natalya looked at her incredulously. "You're going in?"

Kady didn't want to make a big deal out of it. It was just the way things were. And besides, she was grateful for the distraction. "I have to."

The expression on Natalya's face told her that her older sister didn't feel as if that was a foregone conclusion. "You know, you don't have to be super-woman twenty-four-seven, Kady. There're people who can substitute for you. You need to get some sleep, or at the very least, some rest."

There was no way she could sleep right now, even though she was exhausted. "What I need," Kady contradicted, "is to keep my mind busy so I don't think and keep seeing the same scene in my head over and over again." Milos, lying in a pool of his own blood, the dark satin sheets stained a deep shade of red. That was going to remain with her for a very long time, she thought unhappily.

"But if you're sleeping—" Natalya began to argue.

Kady cut her off. "I'll keep dreaming about it. No," she insisted firmly, "my way's best." She wanted to remain so busy that she dropped in her tracks and then, hopefully, had a dreamless sleep.

Retreating, Natalya shook her head. She didn't want to risk upsetting Kady. She'd already been through enough. "You are one of the few people I never could argue with."

Kady could remember some knock-down, drag-out fights that had taken place when they were little girls, fights where neither one of them had emerged the winner. But she appreciated Natalya not giving her a hard time about her decision. She might be the mistress of her own destiny, but her sister could be one hell of a harpy to get around.

"Keep that in mind," Kady said.

She'd almost made it across the threshold and out of the living room when the phone rang.

Kady froze.

By all rights, it could have been any one of a dozen people, maybe more. With three doctors living in the apartment, the call could be coming from the hospital, or from their individual answering services, or even from one of their friends, although this was not a usual time for that. Still, it was possible.

But somehow, Kady knew, knew as surely as she was standing in the middle of her New York City high-rise apartment, that the person on the other end of the line was their father.

Turning around, she saw Natalya already doubling back to the coffee table and picking up the receiver. The sinking feeling in her stomach escalated. It was too late to shout a warning, too late to tell her sister that if it was their father, she was to deny ever having laid eyes on her.

Unable to just walk away, Kady stood, her eyes glued to Natalya, her breath on hold.

"Hello?" It was the last thing Natalya said for a while.

The expression on Natalya's face, plus her silent end of the conversation, told Kady that she was right. It *was* their father. And, as usual when he was agitated, he was doing all the talking.

Retired NYPD officer Josef Pulaski was not generally thought of by those who'd worked with him as an overbearing man, but he was protective of his women. Considering that there were six altogether in his immediate—and only—family, it amounted to a full-time job. One that all of the Pulaski women appreciated, but feverishly, from the bottom of their hearts, wished he wouldn't undertake.

Like now.

Natalya finally ended her silence by saying, "Yes." The next moment, she was holding out the cordless receiver to her. The words were unnecessary, but she said them anyway. "He wants to talk to you."

Resigned, Kady knew that if she didn't take his call now, her father would keep calling back. Or worse, he might decide to have Mama call her. There was never any arguing with Mama. With her father, she had a fighting chance.

Still, Kady placed her hand over the receiver as she took it, giving her sister an accusing look. She didn't need this added aggravation.

"You could have told him I was dead," she whispered, frustrated.

Natalya surrendered the phone. "He would have wanted to see the body," she deadpanned, holding her hands up as if she were backing away from the whole thing. Which she was.

Kady took a deep breath, then blew it out. Trying to manage as cheerful voice as she could, she placed the receiver to her ear and said, "Hi, Dad."

"I was watching the TV," Josef informed her. It

was a given that if he wasn't working at the security firm, or doing something for Mama, Josef loved watching television. He watched everything with the same rabid attention, the news, the myriad of sports channels, dramas, comedies, even commercials. He loved it all. "When they breaking it up with a bulletin."

God bless breaking news, she thought sarcastically. Kady braced herself. It obviously hadn't taken the news media long to pounce on Milos's murder. But then, it wasn't every day that one of the richest men in the country was slaughtered in his own home with his bodyguard not that far away.

"Mr. Plageanos," her father continued, "he is a patient of yours, yes?"

He already knew that. But, like a lawyer building his case, he had to ask.

"Yes."

There was just the tiniest pause. She could visualize his eyebrows knitting themselves together over his patrician nose. "They say his doctor was in the penthouse when he was killed, this is true?"

She waited for the shoe to fall, but for now, she continued playing the game. "Yes."

"Leokadia, that doctor they are talking about, was that you?"

Kady doubted if the media knew yet, otherwise her name would already be splashed all over the channels. But it was only a matter of time. For a split second, she thought of lying, not to spare herself, but to spare him. She knew how her father's mind worked. He'd start coming up with the worst-case scenarios. She fervently wanted to spare them both that. But the dogged news media would undoubtedly learn that she had been the one paying a house call to the billionaire, especially since the practice was completely unheard of these days. And if her father caught her in a lie, he would act as if she'd deliberately taken a lance to his heart and twisted it.

So she was stuck with the truth and all its consequences.

Kady frowned to herself, ignoring her sister, who was watching her intently. Served Kady right for telling her family that Milos had insisted on her being his cardiologist.

Pride goeth before a fall, she thought ironically.

"Yes," she admitted reluctantly.

Apparently it was all her father needed. "Stay there. I'm coming for to take you home."

Stunned, she couldn't believe what he'd just proposed. This was even worse than she thought. "What?"

"I am coming for to take you home," he repeated, enunciating each word because he knew his command of the language left a little something to be desired. "You were at his house. Whoever was killing Plageanos is thinking that you are a witness. That you were watching when this was happening."

Her eyes darted over toward Natalya. There was sympathy on her sister's face. She couldn't hear their father's side of the conversation, but it would take little imagination to fill in the blanks. Had their father had his way, they would have all gone on living at the house where they were raised.

Kady could hear that her father was getting ready to hang up. "Dad. Dad, wait a minute. I didn't see Mr. Plageanos murdered."

For an outwardly simple man, their father was far shrewder than he seemed. He had an innate ability to read between the lines. Life with Mama and her omissions had taught him that.

He wasn't about to be put off so easily. "But you were seeing who did this thing."

Kady sighed. "It's complicated."

"So we make it not complicated. Talk," he instructed. "I am listening."

In the interest of brevity, Kady decided that she needed to tell him everything. Otherwise, she'd be held captive as he asked question after question.

She spoke quickly to keep him from interrupting. "I was in Mr. Plageanos's bathroom when he and his bodyguard were killed. I thought I heard firecrackers going off. When I opened the door to see what was going on, I saw someone I didn't know in the room. He didn't see me," she emphasized. "The man was holding a gun. The bodyguard was dead and Mr. Plageanos was dying."

"Dying?" This was obviously a contradiction to what he'd heard.

"After the killer left, I tried to save Mr. Plageanos. I couldn't."

"Some things are not possible," he told her kindly, then transformed into the protective father who did double duty as a policeman. "This killer, he was not wearing a mask?"

"He had on a turtleneck. He had it pulled up to cover his face, but he let it slip when he thought he was alone."

There was a second of silence, as if her father was digesting what she told him. "And he was not seeing you?"

She could tell that he was skeptical, that he wanted assurance. "No," she told him again.

Her father took a breath. "You are sure?"

Kady paused, then said out loud what they were both thinking. "I'm still alive, Dad." If the man who had killed Milos had seen her, he would have killed her, too.

"Yes," her father agreed with feeling. "And we are keeping you this way."

There was no way she was going to commute from Queens every morning to get to the hospital. She got little enough sleep as it was and that would add an extra forty-five minutes to her commute.

"Dad, I appreciate your concern, I really do. But if I were in any danger, I'm sure the police department would have told me."

She heard him make a dismissive sound. "In case you are forgetting this, I was a policeman for many years. And now I am a security person. *And* your father." Whenever he was trying to make a point, he always felt it necessary to cite his credentials. Kady listened patiently until he got to his point. "Who better to watching over you than me?"

Almost anyone, she thought. She loved him dearly, but whenever he was concerned about them, he tended to get carried away. "Dad, if I need guarding, I'll call, I promise. And I really can't stay at the house. It's too far in case of an emergency—"

"Emergency?" he echoed.

She stopped him before he was off and running. "With one of my patients. I have to be here for them."

Finally she heard him sigh. "Kady, sometimes I am thinking you are as stubborn as your mother."

"Thank you. I'll take that as a compliment."

"I was not trying to giving you compliment."

Her father's voice was weary. She had him on the ropes. Time for a knockout punch before he got a second wind. "'Bye, Dad. Thanks for caring."

"Why should I not be caring?" he demanded. "You are my daughter. Who else am I to be caring for?"

A debate for another time, she thought. God, she hoped Sasha would give him grandchildren soon so her parents' focus would shift. "I'll get back to you on that, Dad. Gotta go."

And with that, she quickly hit the off key before he had a chance to say something more. She put the phone down on the nearest flat surface, not bothering to return it to its cradle. She had a shower waiting for her.

"It's not over, you know," Natalya told her as she followed her out of the room.

Truer words were never spoken. "I know." Kady sighed, beginning to unbutton her blouse. She stripped if off by the time she came to her room. Balling it up, she threw it into the corner. She was thinking of burning it. The blood might come out of the fabric, but not out of the memory.

"It's not going to be over until they catch the guy who killed them." And until that happened, her father would continue to mention having her come to stay in Queens or, worse yet, suggest that he come stay here. The fact that all three bedrooms were spoken for wouldn't deter him. He'd insist on sleeping on the sofa, saying that he'd slept on far worse. And then he'd suffer in silence because he had a bad back.

She didn't want to have to go through that.

Natalya walked over to the corner and picked up the discarded blouse. "Let's hope it's soon."

"Amen to that," Kady murmured. "By the way, throw that out, please," she requested as she walked into the bathroom.

The rest of the day was a blur. Kady saw sixteen patients, three who required simple EKGs, two who were there for their quarterly treadmill tests and one who needed an echocardiogram that had to be re-scheduled because all three machines were mal-functioning or down. There was also an emergency angioplasty for a patient who had the same proce-dure performed by another doctor two months earlier. The artery hadn't been able to sustain the inflation.

She was grateful for the work, even though she found herself tottering on the brink of exhaustion.

But busy as she was, she couldn't shake the uneasy feeling that had her periodically looking over her shoulder. The feeling haunted her for more than one reason. There was a killer out there who might or might not know that he had been seen and by whom. To add to that, her father had accepted defeat far too easily. It just wasn't like him to back off in under an hour.

For all she knew, her father might have decided that he was wasting his breath arguing with her and had just taken it upon himself to play the role of her guardian angel. It wasn't something she'd put past him. To him, *Father Knows Best* was not just the name of a classic 1950s sitcom, it was a creed to live by.

The hairs on the back of her neck bristled more than once when she'd heard a sudden noise, and when her nurse came in unexpectedly, she'd jumped almost an inch off the ground. The nurse had looked contrite and apologized, but the fault, Kady knew, lay with her. She was letting the situation get to her. She had to get a grip. In all likelihood, the killer had no clue as to her identity, and her father was probably busy at work, unable to hover over her. And she, she was letting her overactive imagination get the better of her.

She'd have to work harder to keep it from doing that.

When she came home, both Natalya and Tania were already there.

"Sit. Dinner's ready," Tania told her. When she took her coat, Kady knew something was up. Tania merely smiled sympathetically at her. "Natalya told me."

"About the killer, or about Dad wanting to lock me up in a tower?"

"Both. C'mon," she coaxed, "eat before it gets cold."

Kady allowed herself to be led into the kitchen. She was too tired to be suspicious.

The moment she'd finished eating, or, more accurately, nibbling and pushing her food around on the plate, she excused herself and went to bed. She absently noticed that it wasn't even seven o'clock yet.

Kady couldn't remember the last time she'd gotten eight hours of sleep in the same stretch of time. But she'd fallen into bed and stayed there, sleeping like a rock, until the sound of knocking roused her.

Her eyes flew open, and for a second she felt completely disoriented. Sunlight was flooding the room. Sunlight *never* flooded the room when she woke up. It was always still dark. Where was she?

Lying there, she looked around. She was in her room. Was it Sunday? Her head felt as if it had been wrapped in cotton and her mind felt fuzzy. Her heart was racing in her chest.

A beat later, yesterday came back to her, highlighted with huge neon lights. Oh God, it had all happened. That poor man was dead.

"Kady?" She heard Tania calling through the door. "Are you up yet?"

Kady blinked, then turned her head and focused on the clock on her nightstand. The little hand was on the nine and the big hand was drawing close to twelve. Her heart raced a little faster.

"Oh God," she addressed the words to the door, "please tell me that says 9:00 p.m."

"Sorry," Tania replied, "it's morning. You slept over twelve hours."

Kady leaped out of bed just as Tania opened the

door and walked in. Tania had to be wrong. "I never sleep twelve hours," Kady protested.

Tania shrugged nonchalantly. "Maybe your body had other ideas."

Kady stopped to assess. There was a funny taste in her mouth, and it felt as dry as dust, while her head continued to harbor cotton candy.

"Or someone else did." She looked at Tania. "Did you give me anything?"

Tania was the picture of innocence. "Dinner, as I recall."

Kady tried not to lose her temper. It felt as if everything was beyond her control. "I mean besides dinner. Did you slip me something in my food?"

"You hardly ate your food."

She knew Tania. Her sister was playing with words, hiding behind them. "Okay, then in my drink. Did you put something in my drink?"

"No, I didn't."

She was more than familiar with that tone. She'd used it herself, evading her father's questions. "But Natalya did."

"You'll have to talk to her about that."

Kady was already out in the hall, on her way to Natalya's room. The door was standing open. "Where is she?"

Tania was right behind her. "At the office, like the good pediatrician she is. Shouldn't you be at the hospital?" she asked innocently.

"You know I should," she said between clenched teeth. "Damn, why did she do that?"

Tania spread her hands wide. "I know nothing."

There was a knock on the door and Kady stiffened, braced for the worst. "Get that. And if it's Dad, tell him I'm in too much of a hurry to listen to his bodyguard arguments. Better yet, tell him I've already gone to the hospital—which I would have if one of my sisters hadn't drugged me."

The picture of innocence, Tania saluted and went off to answer the door.

She was back in less than a minute. "It's not Dad," her sister informed her.

Kady tossed a suit on her rumpled bed. If she took a two-minute shower and didn't wash her hair, she could make it in time. "I'm not talking to anyone else."

"You don't have to talk, just get dressed."

Startled, Kady swung around and saw Byron walking into her room. Her first startled thought was that she was a mess. The room was a mess. And he had no right to be here.

It took her a second, but she found her voice. "What are you doing here?"

Trying not to notice that with the morning night shining behind you, the nightgown you're wearing is pretty much see-through, he thought.

Out loud he said, "That composite sketch you came up with yesterday has a match."

Chapter 6

"Who is it?" Kady asked several minutes later as she hurried alongside Byron to the car he'd parked down the block.

She'd thrown on her clothes in record time. To his recollection, he'd never known a woman who could get ready as fast as Kady did. The doctor had gotten ready in fifteen minutes. Her hair was still damp from the shower she'd taken. It gave her a vulnerable look. He tried not to pay attention to the strong pull he felt as he noted the curls at her nape and the scent of soap seemed to surround her.

"Do you know?" Kady pressed when Byron didn't answer her.

He inserted the key into the passenger door. All four locks opened at the same time. "Oh, I know," he told her as he held the door open for her.

Kady felt an uneasiness. Not because her body almost brushed against his as she got into the car. That was something else entirely. But his knowing the suspect meant all of this was close to home. Had it been an inside job? Had someone Milos knew, Milos trusted, been responsible for the ultimate betrayal?

She had to know. "Did Milos know him?"

Kady turned toward Byron as he got in on his side, waiting for an answer. If Milos had known his killer, that would explain why there'd been no sign of forced entry. No cries for help before the sudden attack.

She felt sick in the pit of her stomach at the horrible violation of trust.

Byron wasn't answering her.

"Well, did he?" she asked again, more urgently this time.

Turning the key in the ignition, he glanced at the rearview mirror, then slowly eased out of the spot. A truck narrowly avoided clipping his rear bumper. Morning traffic was like any other traffic in the city. Awful.

"I'd rather not say," he finally told her.

Impatience and confusion rose up in unison. She wasn't at her best in the early hours of the morning.

"Why?"

He glanced at her before looking back to the road. Was that suspicion in her eyes? He wondered what she suspected him of. He had a very logical reason for his silence.

"It might taint the lineup for you."

"Lineup?" She thought she was just going down to identify a photo, look at an array. She hadn't realized it was to view a living, breathing person. Kady's uneasiness escalated as she leaned toward him. The seat belt dug into her waist. "I'm viewing a lineup?"

Byron nodded. From what he'd been told by the police, the suspect had not been an easy man to track down. But then, he would have guessed as much. They'd found him at one of the trendy hot spots, dancing with two women. Once cornered, the man had resisted the idea of coming in and had heaped vile curses on the arresting detectives. He'd been more than a little intoxicated at the time. Word had it that was a common state for the man.

"Best way to make a proper ID," he told her. "I got the call about it early this morning. I volunteered to bring you in."

She didn't understand. "Why? Why did the police call you?" She would have thought that the detective handling the case would have called her. Not that she wouldn't have rather avoided the man and come in with Bryon. "I thought you and Detective Wilkins didn't exactly belong to a mutual admiration society."

"We don't," he confirmed. "But I still know a few guys in the department who owe me favors. I called a couple of them in."

She blew out a breath, trying to make peace with the agitation she felt inside. It wasn't working. It felt as if a blender had suddenly run amok.

With effort, Kady focused on the positive side of what he was telling her. "Looks like you have more support than you thought you did."

Byron spared her another quick glance before looking back at the road. He'd had a feeling she'd catch that. "Looks like," he echoed.

"Why are you doing this?" she wanted to know.

Answering was momentarily postponed as he slammed on his brakes, coming within inches of the side of a van that had shot through a red light. He cursed under his breath.

He took his foot off the brake long enough to get to the next light. "I want to see the old man's killer get what's coming to him. Plageanos was good to me."

Byron left it at that. There was no need to go into how he'd gone into a tailspin after Bobby had been gunned down, or how he'd sunk into the bottom of one amber bottle after another. With Bobby and his wife gone, there didn't seem to be a point to anything anymore. And then one night he'd come to the rescue of a dapper old man coming out of the men's room in an Atlantic City casino. Even two sheets to the wind, Byron couldn't stomach bullies. It later turned out that the men hadn't even known they'd targeted one of the richest men in the world. They'd just seen an easy mark. Byron made short work of the duo and helped Milos to his feet just as the man's bodyguard came running.

Grateful, Milos immediately offered him a job as his head bodyguard, an offer that did not sit well with Ari, his main bodyguard up until that moment. Byron had turned him down, but Milos kept offering. A week later, worn down and with enough time to give the matter some thought, he'd decided to take the job. Temporarily.

Temporarily had turned into three years without any signs of ending. Milos had won him over, and he'd grown to admire him. A great many men in Milos's place would have behaved as if they were entitled to take whatever they wanted. Milos never did. It was more about earning, about hard work.

"I can understand you wanting to find who killed Milos, but that really doesn't have anything to do with being my personal escort to the precinct," Kady pointed out.

He looked at her for a long moment, wondering if she knew how hypnotic her eyes were.

"Does to me," he finally said.

About to protest, Kady decided to let it go at that.

It didn't take a rocket scientist to see that there was no arguing with the man. And if she was being completely honest with herself, she preferred having someone she knew take her in. It made the entire process less intimidating.

She was, after all, looking for a murderer. Someone who had killed not once but twice. Perhaps even more than that. Since she had to confront the killer, it would be nice to have someone she could rely on in her corner. And instinct told her she could rely on Byron.

The room where she stood, looking through the one-way glass at the row of disgruntled men, was small and airless. It was dark and stifling, to the point of being claustrophobic. The size was just a little larger than an old-fashioned phone booth, with none of the light. The only illumination came from two rows of fluorescent bulbs that, on their way to being burned out, took turns winking at each other like flirtatious fireflies.

Kady found it distracting. As distracting as the erratic pounding of her heart.

She took a deep breath of the stale air and tried again.

"Take your time," Wilkins instructed her, himself obviously impatient. She knew he was worried about losing the collar.

As she looked at the lineup, Kady was aware of

the tall, dour man standing to her right. The man in a thousand-dollar suit, whose nails were manicured and whose haircut had cost more than some of the patients she saw at the free clinic earned in a month. The man was a lawyer from some high-powered firm. He belonged to one of the men in the lineup. The suspect she'd seen, she guessed. The other five men in the lineup were probably men in the vicinity of the room who'd been pressed into service by Wilkins. She didn't doubt that some of them were actually policemen.

"This is a waste of time," the lawyer, Jon Reynolds, protested. His suntanned face sported lines of annoyance about his mouth and eyes.

"Don't worry, I'm sure you're getting paid for it," she heard Byron say, his voice rumbling from behind her.

Kady felt better just hearing it. She knew it was probably stupid, but having Byron nearby made her feel protected. She'd seen her brother-in-law, Tony, when she'd come to the floor. He'd been on the far side, talking to someone as they'd approached. Both Sasha's husband and Natalya's fiancé were part of NYPD's homicide division, although they worked out of different precincts. She hadn't realized that Tony worked out of this one. He'd looked at her curiously, and she'd given him an exaggerated shrug.

Had Byron worked homicide as well? she won-

dered. Did he miss being a cop? Or was it nice not
having anyone shoot at you?

"Well?" the lawyer pressed.

"Give her some space," Byron told him. By no
stretch of the imagination could his words be con-
strued as a request.

Reynolds was slightly taller than Byron and
looked down at him. "Why? So she gets whatever
signal you and your buddies here have worked out
in order to finger my client?"

"No, so that she can concentrate," Byron replied. The low tone hardly concealed the barely
harnessed anger.

Kady struggled to block out the drama around
her and focus on her reason for being here. She
looked carefully from one man to the next. They
were all of approximately the same height and the
same coloring. Three had wavy or curly hair just
like the man she'd seen.

They certainly didn't make this easy, she
thought.

Instead of requesting that the men in the lineup
step forward or turn so that she could view each of
their profiles, she was the one who was mobile.
Moving from one spot to another, she studied each
man in turn.

She worked hard at calming herself down. At remembering the small details, the tilt of the head.
The arrogance she'd sensed and witnessed.

"She doesn't know," she heard Reynolds insist flatly.

"No, I don't want to make a mistake," Kady replied curtly, never turning away from the men in the lineup.

She heard Reynolds blow out an annoyed, dismissive breath. "Very admirable, but I think it's time to take my client and—"

"Him," Kady said suddenly, stopping in front of the man who was holding the number three in his hands. "It was him. Number three."

"And where do you recognize this man from?" Wilkins asked, his voice singsongy as he repeated the standard question everyone making an identification was asked.

She turned around to look at the lawyer rather than Wilkins. "I saw this man in Milos Plageanos's bedroom yesterday morning. Just after Mr. Plageanos and his bodyguard were shot."

Wilkins clapped his hands together. "Good enough for me."

"I'll have him out on bail within the hour," Reynolds haughtily predicted.

The assistant district attorney, Lyle Corbett, a small, unimpressive man whose demeanor belied a mind that was constantly working, shook his head. He'd been quiet until now, letting the drama play itself out. Letting Reynolds posture and pose.

But now he had the suspect exactly where he

wanted him, so he smiled, his thin lips all but disappearing. "I wouldn't count on it."

"Who is he?" Kady turned to look at Byron. He could tell her now, couldn't he? Her selection couldn't be tainted anymore. "Who did I just pick out?"

She saw him half smile in amusement. "You don't know?"

Reynolds yanked open the side door and left the small enclosure. He paused only long enough to glare his displeasure at her.

"That's Nicholas Skourous," Byron told her. "Alexander Skourous's grandson."

For a second she drew a blank. And then she remembered. Alexander Skourous. The other shipping magnate. The one Milos had told her had him worried because the man's company was breathing down his neck, cutting into his profits. Trying to damage his good name.

Was this the way the man paid him back for stealing his fiancée? No, that was too far in the past. This had to be about money. It was always about the money.

"I guess Nicholas was trying to level the playing field," she murmured under her breath.

As Kady watched, she saw one of the policemen inside the lineup room dismiss the other men. They filed past another policeman, handing in their poster board signs. All except the man she'd picked out.

Blocked, he began to shout and curse. The look

on his face grew ugly as restraining hands were placed on his shoulders.

"You'll be sorry!" he yelled, looking into the mirror. Looking straight at her. His eyes were wide with fury. "You'll be sorry! More than that, you'll be dead! You hear me? Dead!"

She felt almost as if she'd been physically assaulted. Kady took a step back, bumping up against Byron. Her body brushed along the length of his as she turned to look at him. Though she tried to get herself under control, her heart was hammering so hard she was afraid he could see it. She didn't like being afraid, didn't like being intimidated like this.

She struggled to keep her voice even. "I thought you said he couldn't see me."

"He can't," Byron assured her.

Maybe there was a crack in the mirror, a flaw. "Then why is Skourous glaring right at me? He looks like he's shouting right at me."

"He's not. It's just a lucky guess on his part," Byron told her. He placed one hand on her shoulder, as if to steady her, to reassure her.

She almost shrugged him off. Did he think he had to hold her down?

"I'm not about to bolt," she told him coldly.

"I know that."

If he was lying, he was the best liar she'd ever come across. "Okay," she murmured, then turned to face Wilkins and the A.D.A. "Now what?"

"Now you go back to your life until the trial," Corbett told her in his small, steady voice. Since the word *trial* made most people nervous, he added, "We're going to need you to testify."

She'd already assumed as much before she ever walked into the precinct. Kady nodded, her glance taking in both Wilkins and the A.D.A. "You know where to find me."

Turning, she left the room on legs that felt less than steady. She congratulated herself on making it into the hallway. She wasn't aware of Byron walking with her until they were at the elevator.

"Unfortunately, Skourous knows where to find you, too," he said as he pressed the down button. For a change, the elevator came almost immediately.

The emotionless statement brought a fresh shiver that charged up and down her spine like a cavalry in search of a battle.

She swallowed as the doors closed and they went down to the ground floor. "But he doesn't know that I was the one who identified him."

"His lawyer does."

And his lawyer was bound to tell Skourous. She knew that. Kady pressed her lips together. She couldn't back down. She couldn't do that to Milos. "Okay, well, I'm not going to let him intimidate me."

Byron took her to his car and she got in, feeling

numb. "Is there somewhere you can go?" he asked as they pulled out of the small lot.

She wasn't going to allow some rich, privileged thug, used to getting his own way, to mess up her life. "Yes," she answered simply, raising her chin. "To work."

Stubborn as a mule, Byron thought. But he wasn't about to see the woman rubbed out just because she didn't seem to have the sense she was supposed to have been born with.

"Look, I don't think you fully appreciate what's involved here." He was taking her home for now, not the hospital. And then they could hash it out. "I don't know if the old man is in on it. From what I know about Skourous, he prefers to do his killing in the stock market these days. But this grandson of his, he's a new breed. The kind that doesn't stop at anything to get what he wants. Nicholas Skourous has no honor, no scruples." Stopping at a light, Byron looked at her pointedly. "He killed twice, one more body isn't going to matter."

She brazened it out, hoping that her pounding heart wasn't going to give her away. "You're trying to scare me."

"Damn straight I am," he growled. But the look on her face told him that she wasn't about to listen to reason. Byron told himself he shouldn't have gotten involved. But he had and now it was too late to back away. She'd be on his conscience and he didn't need anything more on that score.

Okay, she thought, so this was serious. But it wasn't just about her. There were more people involved. People who depended on her.

"I *can't* go into hiding, Byron," she insisted again. "I've got patients. The hospital is short-handed. I can't leave them in a lurch. And as for the clinic, there's no way I'm not going there."

The clinic. He wasn't sure what she was talking about, but that didn't matter. What mattered was keeping her under wraps—even if he had to apply the duct tape himself.

"Look, you're not the only doctor in the world. The hospital can—" He got no further.

"Maybe not to the general population, but to some of my patients I am." He probably didn't understand because more than likely he never went to see a doctor, but she tried anyway. "People build up a relationship with their doctor, they form a bond. They give their doctor trust. That's part of their care, part of the healing process." She drew herself up beneath the seat belt, like a warrior about to ride into battle. "I can't just walk away from them."

All that sentiment was well and good, but she was missing a very basic point. "If you get killed, you're not going to be much good to them, either."

Kady blew out a breath that was a little shaky. She hoped he wouldn't notice. "I'll be all right."

"No," he said with feeling, "you won't." And then he thought for a moment. "Unless—"

"Unless?"

The light had turned again. He pressed down on the accelerator. "Unless you get a bodyguard."

They were back to square one. Kady shook her head. "Not a good idea."

"Being dead is better?"

He was painting too black a picture, she consoled herself. "Not everyone who testifies at a trial gets killed."

His laugh was dry and completely devoid of humor. "All it takes is once."

He pulled up to her home. But home wasn't where she had to be right now. She remained in the car. "Look, I appreciate your concern but—"

Byron wasn't finished yet. "I'll be your bodyguard."

Kady's mouth fell open. She sat completely still for a minute. He could have knocked her over with the tip of a parakeet feather. When she pulled herself together, her mind had begun to work again. "I can't afford to pay you." And people like Byron came with a high price tag.

The look he gave her was dark. "Did I ask you for money?"

No, no he hadn't, but the man had to eat. "I can't expect you to do this out of the goodness of your heart."

"I don't have any goodness in my heart," he retorted without emotion. "And this is for Milos. You don't testify, that scum Skourous could go scot-free. That's not acceptable."

This was getting very, very complicated. She'd started out trying to get the clinic a little extra funding and had wound up a potential prisoner. "Look, this is very nice of you, but I just don't have any room in my life for a bodyguard."

"You don't have to make room in your life for a bodyguard," he informed her. "A good bodyguard is unobtrusive, that's their function. I'll take care of the space."

Kady had every intention of being firm, of turning Byron down. After all, he couldn't very well push himself into her life if she didn't want him to. They had laws against things like that. But then she thought of what would happen when her father got wind of this—and he would. He got wind of everything. More likely than not, her father would volunteer to do the same thing that Byron had just offered to do.

The one big difference was that she couldn't put her father in his place, couldn't tell him what to do once he made up his mind. With Byron at least she had a fighting chance.

She slanted a look toward him. "All right." With a sigh, Kady surrendered. For the time being. "We'll work out the terms later," she told him tentatively. "Right now—" she glanced at her watch again "—I'm late."

"Hospital?" he asked.

"Hospital."

"Hospital it is." Byron pulled away from the curb and turned the car in the proper direction.

Chapter 7

Once they'd reached Our Lady of Patience Memorial Hospital, Kady fully expected Byron to stop the car before the front entrance and let her out. Instead he surprised her by driving around the side of the building and going down into the underground parking structure.

The man gave no indication that he was planning to pull over. Instead, he was cruising up and down the aisles, steadily making his way lower and lower into the bowels of the building.

"What are you doing?" she finally asked.

He kept his face forward, glancing from one side to another but not at her. He hated wasting time answering dumb questions and this struck him as a dumb question. "Looking for a parking space."

Warning alarms went off in her head, and she straightened in her seat. "Why?"

She heard him stifle an annoyed sigh. Whether it was directed at the lack of parking or at her she wasn't sure. "Because if you leave a car blocking the flow of traffic, it's going to get towed away."

Was he deliberately doing this verbal dance, or didn't he realize that he was going around in circles? She gave him the benefit of the doubt, although he struck her as too intelligent a man to miss the point. "No, why are you parking the car in the first place?"

"Because it's too big to carry in with me."

Her eyes narrowed. She didn't like the direction this was taking. "And you're going where?"

He spared her one quick glance before resuming the exasperating search. The hospital, he thought darkly, had too many people frequenting it. Which made guarding the woman an even bigger challenge. "Into the hospital with you."

Any hopes that he just wanted to walk her to the E.R. was quickly dying. "No, you're not."

This woman was going to take patience. The challenge wasn't going to be in keeping her alive, it was going to be to keep from strangling her himself. "In order to be a successful bodyguard, I have to guard your body. And since your body is going to be at the hospital, it looks like that's where I'm going to be, too."

He saw a spot and sped up before some compact could dart in from around a corner. "You can't be there," she protested.

"Lady, I can be anywhere I want to be." Byron pulled into the parking space in one long, smooth movement that would have made a stunt driver proud.

Despite herself, Kady was impressed. He was a man of many talents. However, communication wasn't one of them and she wasn't about to have him hovering around, scaring off her patients. Her agreement had been for her off hours. Belatedly she realized she hadn't specified that.

Byron turned off the engine and shifted in his seat to look at her. "What part of bodyguarding do you not understand?"

She was already late. Sitting in the car, debating this was only going to make her more so. Kady quickly got out, slamming the door in her wake as she hurried away from the vehicle.

"I can't have you looking over my shoulder when I'm with patients," she informed him, raising her voice so that he could hear her.

"Doesn't have to be your shoulder." Aiming his remote, he clicked it. The car responded with a little acquiescing noise. All four locks went down simultaneously.

"Doesn't have to be any part of me," she retorted

as he caught up in a few long strides. Annoyed, Kady increased her pace. But even as she did so, she knew that there was no way to outdistance him. The man seemed to be half legs.

"In order to do my job properly," he countered, ignoring the fact that she could easily point out that he didn't actually have a job since no one was paying him for this, "I have to keep some part of your body in sight at all times."

She reached the elevator on the far side of the wall. "So that means you never sleep?" There was more than a touch of sarcasm in her voice. Kady punched the elevator button a little too hard.

Byron leaned against the wall, his body blocking her view of the rest of the area. He was confining her, whether he knew it or not, and she was willing to bet that he did. She didn't like restrictions, never had. She'd gone out of her way as a teenager to circumvent the restrictions her parents had imposed, strictly on principle. She could feel herself rebelling now.

"Usually there are two or more of us on the job and we spell each other."

There were going to be more people cutting into her freedom? She felt adrenaline begin to mount. "This is getting way out of hand." The elevator arrived and she got in. He slipped in right beside her even though she pressed for the doors to close. "And you've been on the 'job,' what?" She glanced at her watch. "Ten minutes." What was it going to be like at the end of the day? Or the week? She needed to put a stop to it now.

"New record," he replied in what she took to be a deadpan. He looked at her as the elevator began its climb up to the ground floor. "It's easier if you don't fight it."

"No, it's easier if you don't do it," Kady countered.

That was not an option. "Like I said, this is for Milos. Besides—" he leaned a hip against the side of the highly polished silver wall "—Milos was fond of you. He wouldn't have wanted anything to happen to you."

"He wouldn't have wanted anything to happen to him, either," she pointed out, "and it did."

The elevator doors opened two floors before the ground. She moved to the side as several people got on and found herself brushing up closer against him than she'd counted on, but there was nowhere to go.

The second the words had come out, Kady realized what she'd inadvertently said. She tried to backtrack. "I didn't mean it was your fault," she continued in a low voice.

She saw his wide shoulders rise and fall. He'd already taken the blame as his own, she realized. Kady felt guilty.

"But it was," he told her in a near whisper. "I shouldn't have gone to talk to the mechanic."

Damn, someday she was going to think first,

talk later. "You didn't expect it to happen in his own bedroom."

That was the difference between them, he thought. She wouldn't have. "But I should have."

"So you're supposed to expect the unexpected?" she questioned. That just wasn't right. "Aren't you supposed to be human?"

The doors creaked open on the ground floor and people began to file out. He waited, keeping his eye on her in case she had any ideas about darting out. Not that he couldn't ultimately find her. When it was their turn, he rested a hand at the small of her back, guiding her out. "On my own time, not his."

She was very well versed in anatomy. So why did five digits resting against her spine create spears of warmth that worked their way up to the base of her neck? "Tall order."

"Yeah."

And he had obviously failed to fill it. Just like he'd failed Bobby. The guilt involved in both pricked like the points of a thousand well-sharpened swords. He'd failed twice. But he'd made up his mind that he wasn't going to fail this woman. Whether she admitted it to herself or not, she needed protecting and he was going to provide it for her. What he'd told her earlier was not just to frighten her, it was the truth. Nicholas Skourous had nothing to lose and everything to gain by eliminating her. There was no way he was going to stand by and let that happen.

She wasn't going to win this. She could tell by the stubborn set of Byron's chin. She'd seen the same look reflected back at her in her bathroom mirror. The best she could hope for was a little give-and-take.

"How about we compromise?" she suggested as the elevator doors closed behind them. The car rumbled as it went back down to levels beneath the surface.

"I'm listening." His expression gave no indication that he had any plans to give even an inch. But at least he was willing to hear her out.

The warmth of the hospital embraced them the second they left the parking structure and entered the building. Kady gave it her best shot, talking fast. "I can't have you there when I examine patients, but you can be somewhere on the floor."

His expression continued to be carved out of stone. "Define 'somewhere.'"

She wanted to go with a broad description, but knew that the only chance she stood was to keep it narrow. She entered the E.R. by the rear entrance. "Anywhere but in the room that I'm using to examine the patient."

"Outside the door." Byron glanced around at the beds that were lining both sides of the hall. Each one was separated from the next not by any kind of a wall, but by fabric. "Or curtain," he concluded.

That was a good deal closer than she wanted, but

Kady supposed she was stuck with it. If she argued too heatedly against it, she had a feeling he'd lose patience with her and she'd lose ground. She sensed that Byron was the kind of man who could only be pushed so far, a man who was willing to be only so accommodating and then no more. She'd save testing his boundaries for another time.

"Those are my terms," he told her when she said nothing.

For just a split second, she thought of pointing out that he had no right to make any terms, but she knew that would be futile. For better or worse, he'd appointed himself her guardian angel and though she wanted to deny it, she had a feeling that he knew far better than she whether or not she needed one.

With a shrug she said, "Then I guess I'll have to accept."

He nodded. "Good move."

She doubted it. But she'd always been one to try to make the best of any given situation. The best in this case was that she didn't have her father hovering around, fussing over her as she tried to go about her work. It wasn't much, but it was all she had at the moment.

The rest of the day was a trial. Kady did her best, but it was a challenge not being aware of him at any given moment. Oh, Byron was true to his word—she never had a doubt that he wouldn't be—

and maintained a working distance between them. But in the final analysis, it was like trying to not be aware of the sun. She didn't have to look straight up into the sky to know it was there. It cast rays everywhere.

It was the same with Byron. Whatever section of the serpentine area that made up the E.R. she was in, Byron was somewhere not too far away. His object, she imagined, was to keep her within screaming distance.

Which was exactly what she felt like doing at least several times during the course of the day. She hated confinement, even consisting of invisible walls.

It didn't help any that several of the nurses had taken note of Byron, a couple commenting on the "tall, dark and handsome" man, wondering if he was a physician from another hospital, or if he'd come in with one of the patients.

"Which of the patients does he belong to?" Patsy finally asked, her question punctuated with an appreciative sigh. Patsy was the youngest of the current E.R. nurses, barely twenty-five. Recently broken up with her boyfriend, her male radar was keenly sharpened.

"He doesn't," the orderly, Jorge Lopez, told her. A newly minted American citizen, Jorge nodded toward Kady as he continued cleaning up after the last patient's mishap with a pitcher of water. "He belongs to Dr. Ski over there."

Ordinarily the abbreviated version of her last name amused her. Today, her nerves tangled together in a convoluted knot, Kady found herself upsettingly short on patience.

"He doesn't *belong* to me."

"Not what I hear," Ray Gilchrist, the chief resident at her side, commented, a wide grin underscoring his words.

Kady shot the man a warning look. "And just what is it that you hear, Gil?"

His smile faded from a face that was liberally sprinkled with freckles and mischief. The chief resident looked at her a little uneasily. No one had ever seen her display any kind of temper or attitude. Like her sisters, she was known for her easygoing temperament. In addition, like Natalya, Kady was also outgoing.

But right now, she was feeling neither. Put upon were the best words to describe what she was experiencing, Kady thought.

"That you're seeing him." The resident's voice was hardly audible.

"Only if I look." Finished inserting an IV into her latest patient, she stepped away from the gurney. The patient was being admitted and she waved Jorge over. "Take him upstairs to the fourth floor." For the patient's benefit, she smiled. "Mr. Carson is going to be staying with us for a little while."

The moment the gurney was wheeled out, her smile vanished.

Patsy didn't seem to notice. Her attention clearly hadn't left the holding cell. "Hey, he's better-looking than the last couple of guys who came around."

The nurse was referring to her last two boyfriends, Kady thought. She believed in having fun and was not in it for the long haul. When it came to dedication, her heart belonged to her profession. It didn't belong to any man and the situation was going to stay that way. Being a doctor required all of her skill, all of her time. Whatever time was left over went to her family. She didn't need a man complicating her life.

"He's not 'coming around.'" Kady stripped off her plastic gloves and deposited them into the wastebasket. "He's on—" God, but this pained her to say out loud "—duty."

"Like a soldier?" Patsy's eyes was literally shining. They'd probably shine if she'd said Byron was a goat herder.

"No, like a bodyguard," Katherine Taylor, Patience Memorial's newest hospital administrator, the fifth in three years, said as she came around the curtain that Patsy was pushing back to the wall. Ignoring Patsy, who looked a little intimidated by her presence, Katherine leveled a long look at Kady. "I had a word with your Mr. Kennedy."

Kady winced inwardly. "He's not my—" Surrendering, she gave up trying to untangle herself from Bryon. The gossips were going to talk no matter what she said to the contrary. She might as well just save her breath. "Oh, never mind."

"Word spreads fast, Doctor," Katherine told her. "So I came to check out the situation myself." The look on her face told Kady the older woman had done more than check the situation out. She'd checked out the man. And, like every other woman in the area, did not find him lacking. "I just want you to know that it's all right if he hangs around, as long as he doesn't get in the way." The woman placed a hand on her shoulder. "We wouldn't want anything happening to you, Dr. Pulaski."

It was obvious that she knew why Byron was here. Had Katherine spoken to him? Kady doubted that he'd volunteer information. Which meant that the woman had another source. Who?

Patsy's eyes grew wide enough to threaten to take over half her face. "Why? What's going to happen to Dr. Pulaski?"

The chief resident was looking at her as well, waiting for some kind of an answer.

She knew that Katherine meant well, but she would have been a lot happier if this had been kept under wraps. The only kind of attention she wanted came from being an excellent doctor who saved lives, not because she'd identified someone who took them. "Nothing," Kady replied firmly.

"And we'd like to keep it that way," Katherine said just as firmly. Then, as if she felt that any major news had to come from her, she said, "Dr. Pulaski was witness to a double murder."

Ray's mouth dropped opened. He had a reputation for being a gossip of the first water. "Not the shipping guy. Play-something-or-other."

"Plageanos," Kady corrected. She glared accusingly over toward where Byron was standing. His expression was unreadable. Okay, she thought, reassessing, so maybe this *did* come from Byron. She turned toward Katherine. "He told you that?"

"No, what he said was that he was your bodyguard. I put two and two together." Katherine did her best to sound sympathetic, but Kady doubted the woman had had much practice at it. "You should have come to me first."

"I didn't come to anyone," Kady protested. "He took this on himself."

The hospital administrator was only half listening. "We have security people here. I can make arrangements so that you can have someone with you at all times when you're at the hospital."

That was the last thing she wanted. Even less than having her father guarding her. "Thank you, but I don't need any arrangements made." Katherine looked as if she was going to protest, so she pointed out the obvious. "I've already got someone with me at all times at the hospital." She glanced toward him again. "Byron seems to think he's a one-man security team all on his own."

"Heads up, Doc, you've got another one," Jorge called out as a patient was being wheeled in through the E.R. entrance.

She was on again, she thought. For now, thoughts of Byron were put on hold.

The word "tireless" was created with someone like Kady in mind, Byron decided.

It was more than a full twelve hours later. He'd discovered that she had an office on the ground floor of the hospital where she saw some of her more regular patients, but for the most part she was in the E.R. handling one emergency after another. To his surprise, she didn't restrict herself only to people whose complaints involved chest pains or shortness of breath. Kady took on one case after another.

Somewhere before eight, an ambulance, accompanied by a squad car, brought in the victim of a foiled liquor-store robbery. At first glance it appeared as if the man, hardly out of his teens, was barely clinging to life. He'd sustained gunshot wounds to the chest and both arms. One shot had missed his heart by less than an inch. There was blood everywhere and, until he passed out, the victim had been screaming. Byron went cold, remembering his brother.

Kady didn't hesitate. She fired off orders like a

drill sergeant, assessing what had to be done and doing it with utmost speed.

The victim's family arrived just as she had stabilized him enough for surgery. She sent the chief resident to bring the victim to the O.R. where a surgical team was assembled and waiting, per her request. Then Kady took the man's wife and brother aside. For the next twenty minutes, she remained with them, answering each and every one of their questions, some more than once, until they were satisfied that they understood what was happening and were assured that everything that could be done for the man *was* being done.

Her attempt to go grab an early dinner, which was in effect a very late lunch, was curtailed by ambulance attendants bursting through the rear doors with two gurneys. One held a father, the second his ten-year-old daughter. Both were victims of a hit-and-run. Kady forgot about eating. All that mattered were the lives that fate had placed in her hands.

When Kady finally came off her shift, he expected her to call it a night and go home. Instead, she went upstairs to check in on the robbery victim and a couple of her own patients who were in the cardiology ward.

Byron felt tired just following her around. But she gave off no such signs as she talked to her patients and to the nurses who oversaw their care.

Hell of a woman, Byron thought.

"You run on batteries?" he wanted to know

when they were finally seated inside his car. Unlike the morning, the parking structure was more than half-empty.

Kady slid her seat belt into its slot. It was past eight and she'd been on her feet forever. But she hadn't realized how exhausted she was until she'd made contact with the seat. It was as if all the air had suddenly been drained out of her. Except for her stomach, which made a protesting noise, as if to remind her that there was very little in it.

"Today was different from most days," she told him. "Most days there's a break."

He figured there'd have to be. Otherwise, she would have been superhuman. As it was, she seemed to be in a class all by herself. Her stomach rumbled again. His mouth curved into a smile. "Want to stop someplace to eat?"

She placed the flat of her hand on her stomach, as if that would silence it. "I'm okay."

"Your stomach," he pointed out, "has a different opinion."

"I'm too tired to chew," she told him, closing her eyes.

She opened them again when she felt him turning. It was too soon to turn. The road from the hospital to the apartment was almost a straight line until the last block. "Where are you going?"

"To put your theory about not being able to chew to the test."

Chapter 8

At first glance, when Kady opened the door to her apartment, it looked as if they were going to be alone. The lights in the living room were all on, but the room was empty. It wouldn't have been the first time her sisters had gone out, forgetting to turn the lights off.

Pocketing her key, she was about to call out to check if either Natalya or Tania were home, but it turned out to be unnecessary.

"I smell pizza," Natalya announced from the next room. The declaration was accompanied by the sound of someone taking in a long, appreciative breath. "If I were a dog," she said, walking into the living room, "I'd be drooling."

Natalya came to a dead stop a few feet past the doorway. Her eyes went from the man who'd been here this morning to Kady and then back to the man. The fact that he was holding an extralarge pizza box did not factor into the wide grin that took over her face.

"Come to think of it…" Her voice trailed off as she tilted her head and pretended to take her time looking him up and down. "Well, hello again," she murmured. "Can't seem to shake Kady, huh?" When he made no answer, she gave him an easier question. "Say, what is your name, anyway?"

He placed the pizza on the coffee table, the way Kady had indicated. He wondered if the redhead was putting him on. He didn't remember her looking this lively, but then, this morning he'd been focused on the fact that a match had been made to the doctor's sketch. That and the way the sunlight had filtered through Kady's nightgown, caressing her limbs like an experienced lover.

"Byron," he finally said.

"Oh." Exchanging glances with Kady, Natalya nodded her approval. Although her heart now belonged to a man whose name was Mike, she'd always had a weakness for names that were unique. Her smile widened. "Like the poet."

"Yeah." He spared Kady a look. What was it with this family and poets? "Like the poet."

Kady nodded at the box on the coffee table. The

rich aroma was filling every inch of the apartment. "Byron sprang for pizza."

"That was very nice of Byron," Natalya said cheerfully. She was already on her way into the kitchen to secure plates and a liberal supply of napkins. "Any particular reason?"

Kady smiled to herself. "The noise my stomach was making was bothering him."

"It didn't bother me." He was quick to correct her, and then he shrugged as if it made no difference to him whether there was misinformation floating around or not. "I just thought that after not eating all day, you'd be hungry."

Natalya was back, juggling a couple of cans of soda and one lone bottle of beer, as well as the plates and napkins. She set everything but the beer on the table beside the unopened box.

"Handsome and intuitive. Nice combination," she commented, humor dancing in her eyes. Natalya handed the beer to Byron. "Here. I thought you might want this."

Byron accepted the beer, but what he wanted was something a lot stronger. What he wanted was to properly toast Milos Plageanos and go off on a bender in memory of the man. But it was just that kind of dead-end scenario that the billionaire had initially rescued him from. If he fell off the wagon now—no matter what the reason—Byron figured that somehow it would be violating the man's memory.

Besides, he wouldn't exactly do the doctor any good if he wound up seeing two of everything before the night was out. So he silently restricted himself to the single bottle he held in his hand.

"Yeah, thanks," he murmured. He unscrewed the cap as Natalya dealt out the plates and napkins and Kady opened the box. She placed a slice on each of their plates.

Within the next half hour, the extralarge pizza was all but gone. Only one lone slice remained in the oil-soaked box. Kady hadn't realized just how hungry she'd been until she'd bitten into her first slice, which was quickly followed by two more.

Hungry or not, she'd eaten less than Natalya. Even after having a full meal, Natalya could pack it away like an anaconda that hadn't eaten for a whole year. Kady had no idea where her sister managed to put it. She always looked as if she'd consumed birdseed for lunch. Of all of them, Natalya had the smallest waist. The word *diet* was not in her vocabulary.

Byron hadn't exactly been a slouch, either, which surprised her. She'd expected him to do little else than nurse the beer and observe them. Instead he'd eaten six slices. Just like Natalya. Except that in her case, eating hadn't prevented Natalya from talking. Byron had used it as an excuse to keep quiet even though Natalya had tried her best to pull him into the conversation at least a dozen times.

"You know," Kady observed, feeling incredibly full and more than a little content as she wiped off her mouth and looked at Byron, "it isn't considered a crime to string together a full sentence." Whenever he had answered one of Natalya's questions, it had amounted to a single-word response. Was he just being closemouthed or deliberately stubborn?

Taking a napkin, Byron wiped off his fingertips again before picking up the bottle of beer. He paused to drain whatever was left. When he set it back on the coffee table, beside his plate, he looked at Kady. "Never thought it was."

Natalya decided that this was a challenge. "Okay, why don't you pick the topic?" she suggested.

"Okay," he answered gamely, then caught them both off guard by saying, "sleeping arrangements."

Natalya looked at Kady. Had she been drinking her soda, she might have choked. Instead she grinned from ear to ear. "Gets right to the heart of the matter, doesn't he?"

Kady shook her head. "It's not what you think, Natalya." It wasn't that she hadn't brought anyone to the apartment to spend the night. There'd been several since they'd lived here. But her quest for a good time had waned of late. Ever since all her efforts to revive Cynthia Applegate had failed. Cynthia had been a young mother with a congenital heart disease. She'd died at twenty-nine, leaving behind an eighteen-month-old son and an inconsolable husband. Cynthia had also left her with a devastating feeling of failure and sorrow. She'd climbed back up on the horse immediately, but six months later she still hadn't been able to shake her sense of sorrow. The only avenue of atonement she saw open to her was to throw herself into her work. That meant no more sleepovers, no more meaningless partying.

She didn't want Natalya getting the wrong idea about this. Since this was only one-third her apartment, Kady felt she owed it to Natalya and to Tania to tell them that there was going to be a man around here for a while and why.

God, it felt weird saying this, she thought. But say it she had to. "Byron is my bodyguard."

The playful expression on Natalya's face all but shouted, "You're kidding." And then slowly it faded to be replaced with a look of concern. Natalya placed her hand on Kady's arm. "Do you need a bodyguard?"

"No," Kady said just as Byron said, "Yes."

Natalya looked from her sister to the pizza-bearing hunk. Afraid of what this could all mean, she tried to keep it light. "So, is it up for a vote? Do I get to cast the deciding one?"

If only it were that easy, Kady thought. "He thinks I need one."

Sitting closer to the edge of the sofa, Byron

leaned forward and looked at Natalya. His was the sort of eye contact that blotted out the immediate surrounding world.

He figured that Kady would want her sister to know. "Your sister identified the grandson of one of the richest shipping magnates in the world as the man who killed Milos Plageanos."

She'd said that he was in the room, not that he had killed the man, but it amounted to the same thing, Kady thought.

Natalya was clearly trying to make sense out of what she'd just been told. She knew that Milos was head of what she'd thought was the largest shipping empire. "So this was about turf?"

That was the simple answer. The truth, once they got to it, was undoubtedly a great deal more involved. "Yeah, in a way. But the important thing right now is to recognize the fact that Nicholas Skourous is a cold-blooded killer who wouldn't hesitate to kill again."

Byron made it his business to get to know the people who figured prominently in Milos's world. He'd learned that Nicholas was a spoiled, self-centered, slightly psychotic bully with a colossal sense of entitlement. Milos had just won a contract that would have helped put the tottering Skourous empire back on its feet had it been awarded to them instead.

"But he's in jail, right?" Natalya looked from

Byron to her sister and then back at Byron again. Neither one was answering her. "Right?" she repeated, this time with more feeling.

"Right," Kady said, then slanted a look toward Byron when he didn't echo her sentiments.

Byron saw no point in sugar-coating it. The woman needed to know what she was up against. One of his former contacts at the precinct had called him on his cell to inform him. "Skourous got out late this afternoon."

"But he killed someone," Kady protested, alarmed. "How can they just let him go like that?"

He'd been through this kind of thing himself more than once when he was on the force. And felt the same frustration he knew she had to be feeling.

"Depends on the judge you draw at the hearing and the nature of the circumstances. You didn't actually see him kill anyone," Byron reminded her. "The judge had him post ten million dollars' bail and surrender his passport."

Natalya laughed dryly. "Yeah, like that's going to do a lot of good. A guy like that can have half a dozen passports made for him by nightfall." She glanced toward the window. The darkness threw their reflections back at her. "By now," she amended. She saw the way Kady was looking at her. "Mike's been educating me about his world," she explained.

Kady turned toward Byron, trying to locate the silver lining in all this. "But that's good, right?

Nicholas's leaving the country," she added in case he didn't understand what she was referring to.

She was clutching at straws, and they both knew it. "*If* he stayed away." He looked at her pointedly. "But you know as well as I do that he's not going to leave a loose end hanging around indefinitely."

Kady could feel her breath backing up in her throat and consciously told herself to calm down. It was going to be all right. "And I qualify as a loose end?" He nodded. She forced a smile to her lips. "First time I've ever been called that."

Natalya strove to find something reassuring for her sister to wrap her mind around. "So you're camping out here with us indefinitely?" she asked Byron. She wasn't entirely sure how this was going to work, or how Kady was managing to pay for all this, but if it kept Kady safe, then she was all for it.

"Just until the trial," Byron clarified. After that he would play it by ear.

"It's either that," Kady added, "or have Dad come live with us."

Like her sisters, Natalya loved both her parents. But distance was a nice thing and a little went a long way. The idea of suddenly having their father living with them on a daily basis was not something she welcomed with open arms. She'd gotten accustomed to her independence and had no desire to feel as if she was ten again.

"Dad?"

Kady nodded. Natalya's tone had said it all. "You know how he is. If he thinks any of us is in danger, he'll be here in a heartbeat."

"Well, you know," Natalya said, glancing back at Byron—nothing wrong with a good-looking man hanging around, being helpful, "it doesn't hurt to be paranoid occasionally."

Kady merely sighed. "I don't know about that."

If pressed, she'd have to say that she didn't like the thought at all. Didn't like feeling as if she needed someone to watch her back, or that there was a need to look over her shoulder every five minutes. Granted she'd grown up in New York, in Queens specifically, and growing up in the city made you street savvy to a degree. But those street-smarts had never interfered with her sense of optimism before, with her general feeling of well-being. She didn't think she had a charmed life, she just didn't think in terms of anything happening to her. Didn't think in terms of being afraid.

This was an entirely new situation she was in, and she didn't like it. Didn't like it because it changed her. Actually thinking that there was someone out there who might want to kill her robbed her of the innocence she enjoyed.

Natalya stifled a yawn. There was no solution readily presenting itself. It was time to table this, at least for now.

"Well, I've got an early day tomorrow, so I'm

going to go to bed." Rising, she nodded at the open box still on the coffee table. "You might want to put a note on that piece of pizza if you're hoping to see it in the refrigerator tomorrow morning," she advised.

He didn't follow. "A note?"

"Yes, saying that the piece is your property—or Kady's if you prefer, but it'll probably carry more weight if you say it's yours. Tania's too polite to steal from strangers." She grinned. "From her own family is another story."

Byron raised a quizzical eyebrow as he turned toward Kady. "Tania?"

"Our younger sister," Kady explained. "Or at least, one of them. There're two," she said in reply to the unasked question in his eyes. "Tania lives with us, but she's away for a few days." She looked at Natalya, who'd obviously forgotten that Tania was going to be gone for a while. "It's a regional exchange program to see how hospitals in other sections of the country are run." That was probably more information than he'd wanted, she thought.

"When she's here," Natalya told him, "she's taken over Sasha's old room."

More names, Byron thought. He tended to take in only what was pertinent at the moment, what had direct bearing on his case. But he had to admit, his curiosity was aroused. "Sasha?"

"Our older sister," Kady told him.

From the sound of it, they were coming out of the woodwork. "Just how many of you are there?"

"Five altogether, counting me."

"And me," Natalya chimed in.

Kady smiled. She was used to people being overwhelmed when they found out just how many of them there were. "Dad says it's more like an army."

He could see why a man might say that. Just being around Kady and her sister gave him a clue as to how frantic things might get. Even exhausted, Kady had more energy than most people he knew. He shuddered, imagining what it would be like, being around five talkative women.

Bobby had been his only sibling and of the two of them, it had been Bobby who was the outgoing one. Bobby who broke the ice anytime something had to be said or brought out into the open. Byron had been the doer and Bobby had been the talker.

God, but he missed Bobby.

"Something wrong?"

Kady was talking to him. Had she been talking long? He didn't usually drift off that way. Looking around, he saw Natalya leaving the room and realized that she'd said good-night.

"Good night," he murmured, as if he were just slow to respond. And then he looked at Kady. She was on her feet, picking up the plates. He gathered up the napkins and the empty cans as well as the bottle of beer he'd had. "Just wondering what it must have been like, growing up in a house with five women."

"Six," she corrected. Putting the three plates on top of the pizza box, she picked it up and headed for the kitchen.

He thought she'd said five sisters. "There are more of you?" he asked, following her.

Setting the pizza box down on the kitchen counter, she removed the plates and put them in the sink.

"There's also my mom." Who was a power unto herself, Kady thought. "I take it you were empathizing with my father." He nodded. "Thought so." Glancing down at the sink, she began to run the water. She squeezed a little hand soap on each plate and quickly washed away any grease. "To answer your question—noisy. It was noisy growing up in a house with six women. Natalya, Tania, Marja and I were always trying to drown each other out."

Marja. He committed the new name to memory before asking, "And your sister—Sasha—she didn't try to drown you out?"

Kady stacked the dishes one by one in the dish rack. "Sasha was always in her own world, way too serious for the rest of us. But in time, we all wanted to be like her, so we became doctors, too."

Five doctors in one family. That took some getting used to. Picking up one of the dish towels that was draped over the oven handle, he started drying the dishes that she'd washed.

"Your parents must have been well-off." It wasn't a question, just an absent observation.

He couldn't have been further off base than if he'd tried.

"Only when it came to love."

Finished, she crossed to the counter and the pizza box. Opening it, she took out the lone slice that sat forlornly on the cardboard and placed it on a small plate. Kady opened the cupboard beside the stove and took out a roll of aluminum foil. She tucked the piece she tore off around the plate and deposited it into the refrigerator. There was no need to label it. Tania wasn't going to be here.

Byron was still trying to add up the numbers. "If your parents aren't well-off, then how…? Medical school is expensive."

She laughed. "Tell me about it." She was still paying off her own loans while helping Tania and Marja with theirs. "By good old-fashioned hard work. My dad was on the police force for years and he picked up work on the side whenever he could. Mama cleaned offices for a while, then did baking and cooking for people in the neighborhood when they threw parties. Every dime that wasn't spent on food, rent or clothing went to the college fund. And as each of us graduated, we tried to help the ones who came after us."

He did the math. "Your last sister has it easy, then."

Marja had her own loans to repay. "None of us had

it easy—but we had lots of love, which makes it more tolerable." She saw a distant look in his eyes, a look she'd seen before in some of her patients. Pain? Longing? She couldn't put her finger on it. And then she remembered what he'd told her about his brother. And how he blamed himself for what happened. Listening to her prattle on about her loving family had to be painful to him. "I'm sorry, I didn't mean to say anything that would make you feel bad."

Byron shut down his emotions, annoyed with himself. He usually kept them under control a lot better than this. What the hell was wrong with him?

Wanting to change the subject and get away from any awkward apologies she felt she had to tender, Byron crossed back to the living room. When she followed him, he was standing by the sofa. "I can sack out here."

Sleeping on a sofa led to backaches, and he was already putting himself out enough. "You could take Sasha's room," she offered.

"I thought you said that your other sister used it now."

"She does, but Tania's not going to be back for a few days at least."

"Plans change. She might come back." He took calculated risks. Being in someone else's bed with the outside chance of having them show up in the dead of night didn't fall under that category. "The couch'll do fine," he told her.

She had her doubts, but she wasn't going to argue. "Okay, let me go and get a pillow and blanket for you."

"You don't have to bother," he called after her as she went to the linen closet.

"And neither do you," she countered. Returning, her arms were full of bedding.

They made the sofa up together. Or rather, he lent a hand, smoothing out a corner while she went about the magic of transforming a regular sofa into a guest bed.

It actually looked comfortable when she was finished. Staying awake, he decided, was going to be a challenge.

"Good night, Byron."

"Good night," he echoed, watching her as she walked away. Her hips swayed just enough to tie up his attention long after she'd disappeared from view.

On second thought, he decided, he was probably going to be up all night. And keeping vigil had little to do with it.

Chapter 9

Byron was on his cell phone when she walked into the living room the next morning, blinking the sleep from her eyes. Thinking for the thousandth time that she was not a morning person.

The sight of him, shirtless and slightly rumpled, had her doing an abrupt mental halt. Stumbling toward the kitchen and more than half-asleep, she'd forgotten for a moment that there was a man sleeping on her sofa.

God, but he looked good first thing in the morning. His muscles looked freshly pumped, rippling with every movement.

It amazed her that some woman hadn't slung

him over her shoulder and run off yet. And then she remembered that he'd mentioned something about not being married anymore. Obviously, the woman hadn't tried to hold on to him very hard.

Byron raised his eyes in her direction. Seeing her, he terminated his conversation with whomever he was talking to and closed his cell phone.

"So you do have a life," she commented, nodding her approval. "I was beginning to worry."

Since he'd come to work for Milos, his job was his life. He didn't know how to do things by half measures. Acting as her bodyguard while doing his own investigation into the circumstances behind Milos's murder was just what he needed to keep him occupied.

He folded the piece of paper he'd been writing on and, rising to his feet, stuffed it into his back pocket. "Just checking out some things on Skourous."

"Oh." The man looked even better standing than he did sitting. It took effort for her to draw her eyes away from his bare chest. She forced herself to walk into the kitchen. "I take it that he's still in the country."

Picking up his shirt from the back of the sofa, Byron followed her. He slid the shirt on and began buttoning it.

"For the time being." He'd put someone he knew from the old days on Skourous's tail and asked to be alerted to any suspicious activity. "He's gone into seclusion at his grandfather's estate in Massachusetts."

She blew out a breath. Massachusetts. It wasn't that long a drive. "Not nearly far enough away."

Kady banished the thought from her head. She didn't have time for this, to dwell on the whereabouts of a man who might want to see her killed. She had more pressing, more immediate matters to attend to.

Opening the refrigerator, she looked in. Everything was as it had been the night before. Natalya had left without eating again.

"Want breakfast? The pizza's still there," she nodded toward the covered plate. "Or I could make you some French toast."

She was already reaching into the refrigerator for the carton of eggs. "You cook?"

The surprise in his voice amused her. "Ever since I could stand on a stool to reach the stove." Her mother had insisted on it. Insisted that they all learn how to cook and sew. You could never go wrong with the basics, she'd maintained.

The laugh was short and full of wonder, as if he was having trouble believing her. "Don't run into many women who cook these days."

She didn't doubt it. "It's a religion with my mother." For now, she pushed the carton of eggs back on the shelf. "I guess she had visions of us gnawing on boxes of frozen TV dinners, starving to death if something ever happened to her. She's so good, Dad's been after her for years to open up her own restaurant."

Sounded as likely a move as any, he thought. The competition was stiff, but the clientele was vast. If her mother was anything like Kady, the woman was bound to succeed. "So why doesn't she?"

Kady grinned, thinking of her mother. "If she had a restaurant, she wouldn't be able to meddle in her daughters' lives as much as she does, and that is her primary passion. My mother is a benevolent dictator, looking for a kingdom.

"But there's hope," she continued. "I think she's been coming around a little more lately. Mama loves getting compliments, even though she pretends to dismiss them, and she really is a fantastic cook." Crossing to the other end of the counter, where all the clean towels and pot holders were housed, she reached in and pulled out a brick-red apron with stencils of appliances on it. Tying the apron on, she turned to look at Byron. "So, what'll it be?" she pressed. "French toast? Pancakes? Eggs Benedict?"

Taking a seat at the kitchen table, he nodded toward the coffeemaker. "Coffee."

She figured him for a coffee drinker. Taking the can out of the refrigerator, she quickly measured out enough for four cups. "And?"

He never woke up hungry, and food didn't agree with him first thing in the morning. "More coffee."

Stubborn, she thought. She put the can back into the refrigerator, then sliced a multigrain bagel and popped it into the toaster. Cooking for just herself was something she'd never managed to work up the energy for. "Breakfast is the most important meal of the day."

"*Black* coffee," he said in a tone that said that was the end of it.

Part of winning was knowing when to stop hitting your head against the wall. Kady backed off. "Okay. We aim to please." She took out cream and sugar in case he changed his mind about the composition of his coffee. And then she looked over her shoulder. "My mother needs to get ahold of you, show you the error of your ways."

"I'm doing just fine."

She tried a different topic. "How did you sleep? Or, better yet," she amended, "did you sleep?"

He never really slept on the job. He'd perfected the ability to sleep with one eye open as the saying went. Never so deeply submerged that he couldn't shoot up to the surface in a moment's notice.

"I caught a wink here and there," he admitted. "Heard your sister leaving."

"Then you weren't asleep," she informed him. He hardly looked the worse for wear. Most men didn't look that good on a full night's sleep, much less five minutes. "She's very good at sneaking out," Kady explained when he looked at her quizzically. "Natalya honed that ability while in high school, creeping out of second-story windows when my parents were asleep. I don't think she got more that ten hours of sleep all told her senior year." Her bagel popped, but she ignored it for the moment. "Look, why don't you go home, get some rest, take a shower, change your clothes." She tried to cover as many bases as she could, hoping to come across something that struck a chord with him. "You can hook up with me later if you feel it's necessary."

They weren't having this same conversation, he silently declared. "It's necessary," he said firmly. "And I am going to get a change of clothes, but not until Mavis gets here."

Both the admission and the new name surprised her. Maybe he wasn't a hundred percent robot after all, she mused. God knew that body of his didn't belong to a robot. Even though he had his shirt on now, all she could visualize were his muscles.

Kady forced herself to focus on the cooling bagel. Taking it out of the toaster, she dressed it in margarine. "Mavis?" she finally asked. "Who's Mavis?"

He eyed the bagel. For a doctor she certainly didn't seem to be concerned about cholesterol. "She was my partner when I was on the force." They'd gone head to head until they'd worked out a rhythm. Mavis turned out to be a great cop. "She left a few months after I did. These days she's in charge of security for a law firm on Wall Street."

Kady didn't understand. Breaking off a piece of

her bagel, she took a bite. "If she's working, her boss isn't exactly going to be thrilled about her taking off to come here."

When Mavis wanted to do something, she always found a way. "Mavis has people working for her. She said it would be no problem and this is just for a couple of hours." Before she could ask, he answered her. "She owes me a favor."

The timer went off. Taking the pot of coffee, she poured the black liquid into a mug that had a bleary-eyed cartoon character proclaiming, "I hate mornings" on it. She pushed the mug over toward Byron, then poured coffee for herself.

"And you're calling this favor in for me?" she asked incredulously.

"No, I'm calling it in for me."

But it was because of her, Kady concluded silently. She didn't want him doing it, didn't want to be beholden to him anymore than she knew she already was.

Kady slid into the seat opposite him at the table. "Look, I appreciate what you're trying to do, but I really think all this is unnecessary."

Obviously, they *were* going to have to have this conversation again. "That's because you don't know people like Nicholas Skourous. I do." He paused to draw in the life-sustaining liquid. Her coffee wasn't half-bad, he thought absently. "Killing you would mean no more to him than killing a fly would to you. The only one who means anything to him is him." He laughed dryly. "He'd kill his own grandfather if the old man got in the way."

There was something in his voice. "You've dealt with him before."

His shrug was vague, careless. "Once or twice."

She shook her head, her cup hiding the smile that came to her lips. "You definitely aren't a man who likes to elaborate."

"No need to." He set his mug down. "You don't need the details, you just need to know that he's capable of killing you without blinking an eye if he feels it's necessary—or if he gets a whim. He killed his girlfriend some years back. Hacked her to pieces in a jealous fit."

Her breath caught in her throat. "Then why isn't he in jail?"

His voice was tight with suppressed anger. "Because the arresting detective got overzealous, bent some of Skourous's civil rights. Evidence wound up being thrown out. And the one eye witness suddenly disappeared." His mouth was grim as he looked at her. "They never found any sign of him."

Kady took in every word, absorbing it, her mind working overtime. Creating scenarios against her will. Scenarios that made her feel ill. "This arresting detective." She measured out every syllable. "Would that have been you?"

Byron paused, grappling with the fresh wave of anger that rose in his throat, leaving behind a bitter taste in his mouth. "Yeah."

Small, small world, she thought. "Hell of a co-incidence."

"Life is just one big coincidence," he told her before draining the last of his coffee. "Most of the time we're just not alert enough to notice."

She couldn't argue with that. She'd witnessed enough coincidences in her life to give Byron's theory more than a little credence. Looking at the empty mug, she nodded toward it. "You want an orange juice chaser to go with that? It's healthy."

He laughed despite himself. "You just don't give up, do you?"

Her smile grew wider. Kady got up and crossed to the refrigerator, as if his answer was already a foregone conclusion. Giving up had never been an option for her. About anything. "Nope."

"Okay. Just not too much." She reminded him of someone who easily took a mile if an inch was offered.

Glancing at him over her shoulder, she gave him a funny little look that he found oddly appealing. "Wouldn't want you to get too healthy too fast," she quipped.

The woman had a smart mouth. Her mouth was also becoming the source of other thoughts.

* * *

Mavis Turner was a heavyset African-American woman, as gregarious as Byron was reticent. She arrived talking and continued to do so all the way to the hospital as she drove Kady there.

She liked her instantly.

It was clear that the woman thought the world of Byron. Kady decided to use this opportunity she'd been given to her advantage. The worst that would happen was that Mavis wouldn't answer her questions.

Kady began pumping the second that Byron left them and got into his own vehicle. "So what's Byron like to be with?"

Mavis pulled out in one wide, daring turn that moved Kady's stomach from its natural resting place to somewhere in her chest. Tires squealing in protest, she tore out of the parking structure and forged a place for herself on the road.

"In the Biblical sense, I wouldn't know." There was a knowing expression on her face as she slanted a look in her direction. A car slammed on its brakes behind them. "If you mean what's it like working beside him eight, ten hours a day, great. You know that he always has your back and any other part that might be sticking out in the line of fire." Mavis sped up, practically crawling up the tailpipe of the car in front of her to avoid missing the light. "I wouldn't be here if it wasn't for Byron. There's nothing I wouldn't do for him."

Kady realized she was gripping the armrest and pried her fingers off. "Would you lie?"

Mavis grunted, as if she'd expected that kind of question and hardly thought it worth her time to answer. But she did. "Don't have to. Byron doesn't like people lying. To him or about him."

Fair enough, Kady thought. But then, could she expect anything less from someone who called herself Byron's friend? She decided to change the direction of her questions to something a bit more social. "Does he have anyone in his life?"

Mavis shook her head. "Most solitary man I've ever met." She paused, as if debating. And then she said, "There was someone a while back. Rebecca or Rachel. Something with an *R*. He was married to her eight, ten months," she added casually.

The name wasn't important. The circumstances, however, were. She told herself she was only satisfying idle curiosity. "What happened?"

"The whole thing fell apart after his brother was killed." Mavis had told her earlier that she was married with three children and felt that everyone needed that kind of stabilizing home life to come home to. "He pushed her away. Pushed everyone away. Except me." She chuckled, glancing down at her ample lap. She more than filled her seat. "You might have noticed, I'm not exactly the pushable size. I wouldn't budge.

"'Sides," she continued, "he reminds me of my little brother, Mel. Except that Mel's happy." She shook her head. "There's a whole lot of hurt inside that man. The right woman for him would be one who could stick it out. Who's not pushable," she emphasized.

They were here already, Kady realized. She'd never made it from her apartment to the hospital so fast. Engrossed in what Mavis was telling her, she'd forgotten to white-knuckle it.

As they pulled into the parking structure, Mavis began to cruise, looking for a space. She was still whizzing by. "What's your story?"

The question caught Kady off guard. She looked at the woman in the driver's seat. "Excuse me?"

Mavis gave her the long version of her question. "Why do you need him guarding you?"

Kady was surprised. "Didn't he tell you?" She would have expected him to elaborate in order to get the woman to agree. But then, friends did things just because they were asked. She would, if any of her sisters needed her.

Mavis was traveling down another aisle, still searching. She shook her head. "All he said was that he needed a favor for a couple of hours."

It was obvious but Kady still marveled. "And you just dropped everything?"

Mavis glanced at her. "This is Byron. He don't ask 'less there's a reason. So what's the story?" she asked again. "Why do you need a bodyguard?"

Kady didn't want it to seem as if she was the one who'd asked for this. "It was his idea."

If she meant to get sympathy, she failed. "He doesn't have them unless there's a reason."

There was no sense in being secretive. The story was undoubtedly going to be in the paper today. Not to mention splashed all over the TV screen, probably for weeks to come. Every time the media caught hold of a story that involved the demise of anyone remotely famous, it sank its collective teeth into it and hounded the details to death.

"I was in his penthouse apartment, in the next room." Saying it was the bathroom somehow seemed to trivialize what she'd witnessed. "When Milos Plageanos and his bodyguard were killed."

Mavis stopped driving to stare at her. The two drivers behind her immediately began to lean on their horns. "That was you?"

"Yes."

Mavis started driving again. To Kady's surprise, the woman chuckled. "Damn, girl, you should sue the media for that picture they ran of you."

An unflattering photograph was the least of her concerns. Someone had leaked the information to the press. Which meant that even if Skourous's lawyer hadn't told him who the witness against him was, the newspapers had. She slumped against the back of the seat. "That's not exactly on the top of my list of things to do."

"Gotcha." Tires squealed again as she sped up, her eyes on the space she'd located. One sharp turn later, they were in the space. "First thing's always to keep on living."

Which wasn't easy, sitting in the passenger seat of a car that Mavis was driving, Kady added silently.

After they got out of the car, Mavis locked all the doors with the press of a button, then took a deep breath. It was followed by a sad shake of her head.

"What's the matter?" Kady asked.

They began to walk toward the elevator. "Smells like a hospital already."

Kady stared at her, astounded. "We're just in the parking structure."

"Makes no never mind," Mavis insisted. "I can smell the rubbing alcohol and ether clear down to here."

Mavis was more than twice her size. Kady decided that it might not be the most prudent thing to point out that what the former police detective was saying was physically impossible.

"You're kidding, right?"

After almost a week of playing her silent shadow, he thought he knew her whole routine. He hadn't imagined in his wildest thoughts that her weekly routine included spending time in an unsavory neighborhood every Friday afternoon. He knew about the clinic, but this...

She'd just finished making her final notes and had given the patient's chart to the attending nurse. With that, she took out her medical bag and informed him where she had to go next.

"No, I'm not kidding. Should I be?" Opening her bag, she checked to make sure she had everything.

"Damn straight you should be." He could see by her expression that he'd lost her. "Are you insane? Why the hell would you want to go waltzing into Spanish Harlem of you own free will?"

She began to walk toward the bank of elevators, resenting his tone, resenting the fact that he was treating her like an addle-brained child. "Well, for one, I'm not waltzing. I assumed we'd drive over. If you don't want to drive me, I can take the bus or borrow Natalya's car. She hardly ever uses it."

He was beginning to wonder how this woman had managed to avoid getting killed up to this point. Angry, he followed her down the corridor. "Why Harlem?"

"Because that's where the clinic is."

He frowned. Didn't she realize how risky it was, going there? "You work at the hospital."

"Yes," she agreed tersely. The elevator arrived and she got in, pushing the button for the underground parking. "But I also volunteer at the 125th Street free clinic on Fridays."

He let out an exasperated sigh. "Can't someone else do it?"

She hadn't expected that from him. Maybe she'd misjudged the man after all. "That's the sad tagline that allows everyone to turn a blind eye and ignore people who need them."

Charity was fine, but he was trying to keep her alive, and she wanted to go to what was a daily war zone. "Don't you know it's dangerous going up there?" He didn't add that her pale complexion and light-blond hair would make her stand out in that neighborhood. Like a target.

The doors parted again and she began walking in the general direction of his car.

"What's dangerous is that if it wasn't for the clinic and the doctors who volunteer there, the people in that area would never get any medical treatment at all. It took me a while to get my patients to trust me. I'm not going to abandon them now because some rich psychopath *might* try to kill me."

"I wasn't thinking about the rich psychopath," he growled. "I was thinking about the poor ones." He gave it one more shot. "You're walking straight into gang territory. There're drive-by shootings during the day. Not to mention rapes."

If he meant to scare her, he failed. She'd known all about the dangers when she'd signed up. All she focused on was that she was needed. Badly. "And the victims of those drive-by shootings and rapes need me," she insisted. "If they don't get medical attention, they die."

He could either walk away or take her where she wanted to go. It was obvious she was going in either case. "Ever think about going into politics?"

"Why?"

His mouth twisted cynically. "Because you have an answer for everything."

She met his cynicism with a smile. "I grew up with four sisters and a very strong-willed mother. I learned to debate and hold my own *very* early in life." She looked at him. It was getting late and she had to get going. "So, are you coming with me or do I go alone? Because either way, I am going."

He knew that. They'd shared almost a week together. It hadn't taken him that long to discover that he had chosen to stand guard over one of the most stubborn creatures who had ever walked the earth.

"If you're determined to hang a target sign around your neck, you're going to need someone watching your back—and your front," he grumbled. "So, yeah, I'm going with you." He pointed toward where his car was parked. "Just how long are you planning on playing Albert Schweitzer today?"

"Barring an emergency, my shift ends at eight."

"Eight," he repeated. That made for another marathon day. The woman really did run on batteries.

"And just for the record," she added, getting into the car, "I'm not playing."

Chapter 10

At first glance, it looked like just another store-front shop, here today, gone tomorrow. But special touches provided by Milos's contributions set the clinic apart. It was situated in the middle of a long city block, housed between a green grocer and a store whose owner promised to unlock the secrets of the world by gazing at your palm.

Byron parked in the tiny lot located behind the building half a block away. He gave serious thought to just locking all four doors and driving away before Kady could get out. He didn't like the looks of the neighborhood. Seedy, rundown and littered with vagrants, it wasn't the kind of place you brought someone like Kady to.

But this was her life; he was just along for the ride. So Byron parked his car and got out. His senses heightened, he carefully scanned the area.

"This is a mistake," he told her.

"It's what I do," she countered with a smile that he found almost unbearably sweet. The woman was something else. Right now, he didn't trust himself to elaborate on what that "something else" involved.

Keeping his body between her and the street, he hurried her to the clinic.

From what Byron could see through the surprisingly clean bay window as he brought Kady up to the door, there appeared to be standing room only inside the newly renovated clinic.

Opening the door and walking in didn't alter the impression. The small reception area was jammed with people, all waiting to be seen and treated. Mostly there were mothers with their children. Here and there, Byron saw a few men, their backs literally against the wall. Byron estimated that there had to be twenty, thirty people in the limited space. Maybe more.

And they were all waiting to see the "doctor on duty."

It was a hell of a tall order.

Byron looked at Kady uncertainly. "You're going to treat all these people?"

She took a breath before answering. "I'm going to try."

She'd told him that the clinic's doors closed at eight. He didn't see how all these people could be seen by then. "How many other doctors are there here?"

Byron looked round, looking for another doctor amid the tired, drained, sometimes arrogant and resentful faces he saw.

"There are no other doctors here today." He looked at her sharply. "Just me."

Cristina, a nurse-practitioner whose diploma was only nine months old, had been holding down the fort all morning, treating as many people as she could. The slim, dark-haired young woman walked out into the reception area to call the next patient. When she saw Kady, Cristina's face immediately lit up.

"Thank God," she said loudly enough to be heard above the din of voices.

"This is crazy," Byron commented as they threaded their way to the rear of the clinic and the two examination rooms located there.

"Tell me about it."

But she knew that he was only commenting on her being up to this much work. She was referring to the fact that these people shouldn't have to be put in this kind of position in the first place. There should be more clinics like this one in the area. More doctors who were willing to give of their time. Her sisters all volunteered here, as well as a number of other doctors they had managed to coax and cajole into coming. But it wasn't nearly enough. Just a drop in the bucket.

She forgot about Byron for a moment as she began greeting people whose faces had become familiar to her. Just as she was about to go behind the reception desk, a woman with gray streaks in her hair grabbed her arm. When Kady turned to look at her, the woman pointed to the small boy with her. Dressed far too thinly for the weather, the child, a boy of six or seven, seemed to be radiating heat. His face was flushed and he was perspiring.

"Doctor, please," the woman pleaded in a heavily accented voice. "Roberto sick."

Byron, thinking that this might be some sort of trick to distract her, began to step in between Kady and the woman. Kady waved him back, her attention focused on the child.

As he stood there, feeling oddly impotent, Byron heard Kady gently ask the boy what he was feeling in Spanish. Roberto looked up at her with eyes that were watery and glazed. His breathing was labored as he uttered a single word. *"Malo."*

"Cristina," she called over to the young woman. The latter had stopped to pick up the sign-in chart and was bringing it over to her. Making a judgment call, Kady disregarded it for the time being. "We need to get this boy in first."

All around her, voices rose up in protest.

"I was here first."

"Hey, that's not right."

"Yo soy primero."

Byron moved even closer to Kady, slipping his hand in beneath his jacket as he reached for his weapon. The situation looked as if it would get ugly. Usurping whatever order might have been created was liable to lead to chaos with this crowd. She should have realized that.

"You're going to have a riot on your hands," he warned, trying to move her toward the back. Anger was a great motivator, especially among people who'd been deprived and ignored for most of their lives. It would take little to set them off. He'd seen more than his share of this kind of thing when he'd carried a badge.

When he put his hand on her shoulder to draw her back, Kady shrugged it off. Rather than retreat out of fear or what he felt was common sense, she seemed determined to stand her ground. Raising her voice, she addressed the people in Spanish.

Byron knew just enough of the language to catch a few phrases. She was explaining why she was taking·the boy in first, playing on their sympathies.

Byron curled his fingers around the hilt of his gun. Just in case. To his surprise, the people quieted down, and the keen resentment that seemed to be churning in every space dissipated.

Leaving his weapon holstered, he followed Kady

to the back. He couldn't help thinking that they could have used her in crowd control back in the old days. "How the hell did you do that?"

"You can do a lot with compassion," she told him simply. "And by treating people with respect and dignity, as if they matter."

He wondered if that last comment was directed at him. But the expression on her face didn't hint at any hidden agenda. Byron decided that maybe he was a little too thin-skinned at times, despite his efforts to harden himself against everything.

Kady knocked on the door to the first exam room. He was about to follow her in, but she turned around and placed her hand on his chest, pushing him back. For a small woman, she had a lot of strength.

"I need to see my patients in private," she reminded him.

Byron frowned. That was all well and good at the hospital, but out here, in no-man's-land, it was another story. There was no metal detector in the doorway, no one to make the people who entered the clinic surrender their weapons at the threshold. Who knew what kind of an arsenal made it into the clinic?

"Right...but—"

She pushed her hand against his chest even harder, shaking her head. "No 'but.'" And then she added, "If I need you, I'll holler. I promise."

As far as he was concerned, that was not a compromise. "Might be too late by then."

"Might not," she countered with a smile, then shut the door.

Byron stood glaring at the barrier. She was easily the most frustrating woman he had ever dealt with. It would take very little effort to bring the door down if he wanted to. For a second he debated doing just that, then gave it up. Swallowing the curse that readily rose to his lips, he dragged a chair from behind the minuscule reception desk, bringing it into the crammed corridor. He planted the chair and himself next to the closed door.

And waited.

Time dragged by in slow motion as patient after patient came in and had their turn with the doctor.

Byron continued to sit in the hall. From his vantage point, he could see the front door and the people who came through it, as well as the ones who were brought to the exam rooms.

He would have become terminally bored were it not for the periodic jolts of adrenaline that shot through his system each time someone with clear gang affiliations came into the clinic.

It felt as if the night would never end.

When he looked up at the black-rimmed, white-faced, old-fashioned clock that hung on the wall above the small reception desk, it had finally turned eight.

And then eight-fifteen.

And then eight-thirty.

The front door had been locked a half hour ago. He'd done the honors himself, opening it again only long enough to allow each of the last patients to leave, one by one.

Eight thirty-five, Kady and the nurse-practitioner, along with the grandmother who had brought in two of her seven grandchildren, came out of the second exam room. Kady walked the woman and her grandchildren to the door and unlocked it herself. Smiling at the children, she bade the woman good-night.

Breathing out a long sigh of relief, the nurse-practitioner waited until the woman and her children were safely out the front door, then grabbed her things and headed for the door herself.

"'Night, Doctor." Cristina nodded at Kady, then looked over toward Byron. It was clear that after half a day, she still didn't know what to make of his presence there. "'Night," she murmured. The next moment she was out the door and gone.

That left the two of them. He studied Kady. It was hard to believe that the petite blonde was such a dynamo, but there was no other way to describe her. Other than incredible. He could see why Milos had been so partial to the woman. There was an energy about her. And she cared. Hell of a combination.

He crossed over to where she was standing at

the reception desk. She was making notes on someone's file.

"Can I take you home now?" he asked. "Or do you have a third-world country you need to save?" He'd meant for the words to be sarcastic, but some of the admiration he'd come to feel for her had slipped through.

The smile was weary, but it rose up into her eyes. He caught himself thinking that she was beautiful.

"You can take me home." She finished making her notations and closed the folder, putting it on top of the stack that sat on the counter. There was only a fifty-fifty chance that it would be filed away tomorrow. "You know," she commented, coming around the desk, "you're not nearly as tough and hard-hearted as you'd like everyone to believe."

He knew better than to argue with her. He had a feeling that even weary she could still argue the ears off a brass monkey and he was way too tired for a sparring match. It was dark, and all he wanted was to get her out of here and safely home again.

Byron wondered if he'd find his car where he'd parked it. And if the wheels were still on it. Again he couldn't help thinking that there were safer ways for her to spend her time. And a lot safer places.

"If you say so," he muttered.

Just then he heard the door open. Belatedly he realized that neither one of them had flipped the lock when Cristina had left. He roundly cursed himself for assuming they could make it out the door before anyone showed up.

"We're closed," he said gruffly, turning toward the door.

The moment he did, he found himself looking down the barrel of a gun.

"No, you ain't. You just opened up again."

The person brandishing the weapon was hardly more than a boy. Eighteen at most, maybe younger. His head was shaved, there were a number of piercings on his face and along his body. The tattoo on the side of his neck proclaimed him to be a member in good standing of a local gang.

Byron moved so that his body was between the gun owner and Kady.

"There's no money here."

It surprised Byron how calm Kady sounded. He would have thought that facing the business end of a revolver would have frightened her. But then, he'd come to expect the unexpected from her. Apparently she was a woman who didn't fall apart in an emergency. His admiration went up another notch, even as he tried to assess the situation and how to disarm the young thug.

"Think I don't know that?" the thug scoffed. He paused a moment to brag, to impress them with his credentials. "I know everything that goes on around here." With a toss of his head, he jerked a thumb at his chest. "This is my turf."

"If you don't want money, what the hell do you want?" Byron demanded.

The teenager's eyes narrowed into angry slits as he waved his gun at him. "Don't be givin' me no attitude," he snarled. "I can put a bullet right through you just like that."

Kady bridled her horror, but she was still afraid that the teenager might feel challenged and do exactly what he said. She couldn't just stand by and see Byron get shot, especially since the only reason he was here was because of her.

She moved out of Byron's shadow. "What's your name?"

The question caught him off guard. "Juan. Like the number Juan," he exaggerated the sound to make one and Juan seem identical.

"What do you want, Juan?" she asked, repeating Byron's question, omitting the snarl but not the authority. She made a point of looking Juan straight in the eye.

Juan shifted his weight to the balls of his feet, as if expecting a fight. His eyes darted toward Byron's face before looking back at her. "I need you to help Lucy."

Out of the corner of her eye, she saw Byron moving forward. Damn it, was he determined to get hurt? She had no doubts that Juan's gun was loaded and that the teenager would kill him as easily as he'd scratch himself. She put her hand out to keep Byron in place, her attention never leaving Juan.

"Is Lucy sick?"

"Sick? Hell no, that was months ago." The laugh he uttered was dismissive. "She's about to pop, that's why you gotta help her."

Kady quickly put two and two together. "She's pregnant?"

Juan wiped his forehead with the back of his hand. *The kid's scared*, Byron thought. He calculated how to disarm him. He didn't want to risk the gun going off and having a stray bullet hit Kady.

"Not for much longer," Juan told her.

Moving back behind the desk, Kady pulled her bag out where she'd left it. She assumed that he was going to take her to Lucy. "Where is she?"

He nodded his head back over his shoulder. "Got her in the car. Can't you hear her screamin'?" he asked incredulously. "Nearly made me crash, getting here. Lucky no cop stopped me."

Kady was already at the window, looking out. There was a beat-up black vehicle, as old as the wheels were new, at the curb, parked sideways. She could just make out the young woman in the passenger seat.

She looked back at the teenager behind her. "You need to get her to a hospital."

Juan lost no time getting to her. "I need to get her to you!" he corrected hotly.

It wasn't a good idea. There were all sorts of complications that could arise, especially in a first-time pregnancy for what she assumed had to be a teenager. But she knew before she even opened her mouth that she wouldn't get anywhere trying to reason with him. He looked too volatile—and too scared.

"Byron, I need your help," she said.

She sounded a hell of a lot more calm than he was feeling right now. He heard the gun being cocked behind them. He worked at holding on to his temper. "What do you want me to do?"

"Help me get her out of the car." Not waiting for a response, Kady hurried out of the clinic and toward the vehicle.

Byron followed her to the car. Kady was already opening the door. The girl in the front seat looked to be about sixteen. She was contorted with pain and there was fear in her eyes.

"Lucy," Kady said gently, "I'm Dr. Pulaski. I'm going to help you have your baby."

Lucy grabbed her wrist, holding on in a death grip. "Cut it out of me," the girl begged. "I don't want it no more. Cut it out! Please!"

Her body grew rigid, and the girl let loose with another blood-curdling scream. If she had been on Sixth Avenue, everyone would have started running. But Byron knew that in the neighborhood where they were, gunfire and screams were sadly an everyday occurrence.

Moving Kady aside and ignoring Juan, who was ordering them to "do something," Byron tried to draw the pregnant teenager from the passenger seat. She was in too much pain to stand. Resigned, Byron bent down and picked her up. Turning, he began to carry the sobbing girl back to the clinic.

"Hey, you carry her right," Juan ordered. "That's my woman you've got. No funny stuff."

"Don't worry about it," Byron told him, his voice steely. Once back inside the clinic, he looked at Kady. "Where do you want her?" He raised his voice at the end of his question to be heard over Lucy's screams.

Kady was quick to lead them to the larger of the two rooms. "Right here in the back. Put her on the exam table."

As he did what Kady told him to do, Lucy's screams rose to a level that would have had dogs wincing.

Chapter 11

Juan's dark eyes darted from Kady to Byron. "You gonna help her, right?" the teenager demanded. "Right?" he repeated, his voice growing progressively more agitated.

"Right." Byron answered him before Kady could, his voice emotionless as he placed Lucy on the table. Straightening, he looked Juan directly in the eye. "And you're going to help by putting that gun away." It wasn't a suggestion. "Now."

"Not until you get this kid out," Juan countered nervously, pointing at Lucy's round belly with his free hand. Both men were shouting to be heard above Lucy's screams.

"I'm a doctor," Kady informed him, placing her body in between Juan and Byron. "I don't need to have a gun held to my head in order to do what I'm supposed to do." Her eyes narrowed. She didn't need more people to patch up tonight. "Now you put that damn thing away before you hurt somebody."

"You can't talk to me like that."

"Please," Kady added.

Juan shifted angrily from foot to foot, breathing heavily. The expression on his face was dark and malevolent. But in the end he cursed and stuck the weapon in the front of his waistband, the gun barrel pointed downward.

Byron eyed the gun in its new position. The slightest wrong move and it was going to go crashing to the floor with who knew what results.

"Unless you want to shoot something off, I'd suggest you put your gun on the counter over there." He nodded toward the narrow ledge that ran along one wall.

Juan looked more inclined to use the gun than to relinquish it, but he did as he was instructed.

Trying to hold down a very uncooperative Lucy, Kady looked from one combatant to the other. "If we're done with the O.K. Corral reenactment, I could use a little help here."

It was apparent that her reference was lost on Juan, but he attacked the heart of her statement.

"What kinda help you need?" The request mystified him. "You the doctor."

"I need someone to hang on to Lucy's hands and hold her down so she doesn't fall off the table." Lucy was waving her arms around, trying to distance herself from the pain. She continued to bellow at the top of her lungs. Kady stepped back, and the two men took her place. "If your baby has half the lung power that you do," she told Lucy, "you're going to have yourself an opera singer on your hands."

"Don't want no opera singer," Juan declared, sneering at the very thought. "He's going to be tough, like his old man."

Lucy didn't appear to hear any of the dialogue. She was too busy cursing everyone and everything, including Juan.

With Byron holding Lucy down on one side and Juan struggling to hang on to her on the other, Kady hurriedly took out a fresh pair of surgical gloves and pulled them on. "I know this isn't comfortable, Lucy, but it'll be over with soon enough."

"Now. Get it…over with…*now!*"

Kady tuned the teenager out as she got down to business. She pushed aside the girl's loose blouse and started to remove the girl's sweatpants when Juan caught her wrist, holding it hard. "Hey, what you think you're doing?"

Kady glared at him. Juan bit off a curse and released her wrist.

"You watch that mouth of yours," Byron told him evenly. "Or you get to watch your kid being born from a hole in the roof that you personally would have made with your butt."

"I've got to see how far along she is," Kady quickly explained, hoping to forestall any kind of violence.

Juan glared at Byron, his nostrils flaring. "What about him?"

Catching on, Byron answered, "I only look where she tells me to look." He deliberately looked over Lucy's head.

For the moment Juan appeared placated. But the next second he was being jerked down as Lucy pulled hard on his arm, screaming loudly again.

"Damn, woman. One more move like that, and I'm leaving, hear me?"

Lucy began to cry. "Don't…go…don't…go."

"He's not going anywhere, Lucy," Kady soothed. "This your first baby?" she asked, trying to distract the girl as best she could.

"And…last."

Sasha had told her she'd heard that promise more than a few times before, Kady thought, suppressing a smile. Moving quickly, she took the pregnant teenager's sweatpants and underwear off, then spread a blue paper sheet over her. She positioned it so that the only area that was exposed was what she needed to see.

"She's dilated to a ten."

Juan stared at her. She might as well have said something in Latin to him. "What's that mean?" Juan demanded.

"It means you're going to be a daddy very soon," Byron told him. He'd had a training course that covered this when he was just on the force. He didn't remember much, but he did remember that ten was the magic number.

Frightened, Lucy started screaming again, even louder than before.

"Calm down, Lucy," Kady ordered. "Calm down." She didn't want the teenager using up her energy.

"Give…me…something!" Lucy pleaded. "Give… me something…for…this…pain. I can't…take… it…no more!"

"Me, too," Juan said suddenly. "I could use something for the pain."

"Suck it up," Byron ordered the young gang member. "You're not getting any drugs."

Kady took hold of Lucy's hand for a moment. "I can't give you anything right now, Lucy. I need you conscious and focused for the baby."

"Let…the damn kid…focus…for…himself," Lucy sobbed. Suddenly she arched, nearly tumbling from the table. Byron grabbed her just in time, holding her steady.

"Hold her down!" Kady ordered, directing the command to Lucy's boyfriend.

"Doin' the best I can," Juan snapped back. He looked down at Lucy's contorted face. Her long black hair was plastered to her forehead. Leaning his weight against her arm to keep her steady, he used his free hand to push back the hair from her face. "C'mon, Luce, you can do this."

"You…wanna…take…my…place?" she snarled.

"Listen to your boyfriend," Kady told her, doing her best to keep her own voice low-keyed. She'd quickly gotten what she needed ready on a tray. "You can do this. Your mother went through this. Your grandmother went through this. You can do this. You—" she looked at Juan "—get behind her back and raise her up. Right, like that," she coached when he awkwardly pushed Lucy's shoulders forward. Kady sat down on a stool and positioned herself between the girl's raised legs. "Now I need you to push, Lucy. On my count, I want you to push. One, two—"

She didn't get to three fast enough. Lucy was screaming and crying, pushing as hard as she could.

"Okay, now stop. Stop!" Kady ordered. Juan backed away and Lucy collapsed against the table, panting.

"Why're you makin' her stop?" Juan protested. "The kid ain't out yet."

"I need her to save some of her energy," Kady explained. "Or else she's not going to be able to push the baby out. This happens in stages." She didn't have the teenager hooked up to a monitor. There was none to be had in the clinic, but she could tell by the rigid way Lucy's belly was contracting that that another contraction was on its way. "Okay, here comes the next one. Push, Lucy, push!"

Juan quickly propped her up again.

"I…am…I…am!" Lucy screamed, then sobbed as she fell back before Kady told her to. "Why… isn't…it…coming…out?"

"Just a few more minutes," Kady promised. "The baby will be out in a few more minutes." She could see the head, it wouldn't be long now.

"I'm…gonna…die…in a…few…more…minutes," Lucy panted, sobbing.

Kady raised herself on the stool, her eyes meeting Lucy's. "No, you're not," she said sternly. "You're going to live and have a beautiful baby." Lucy's belly was growing rigid again. It was time. "Okay, get ready. Get behind her and prop her up again, Juan," she instructed the teenager. Juan looked completely drained and bewildered. She didn't have time to reassure him, as well. There was a baby fighting to be born. "Now push! Push! Good, you're doing good! Here comes the head."

"The head?" Juan looked out from behind his girlfriend. "Where the hell's the rest of him?"

"Coming, he's coming." Kady kept her eyes on the tiny being who was emerging. She had a towel ready just beneath his head, drawing him out as he came. "We just have to clear the shoulders." Even as she was intent on this brand-new life coming into the world, she was aware of Byron beside her. Watching all this. Being part of the miracle she was privy to. It made her suddenly feel close to him.

"Can't...you...just...yank him...out...now?" Lucy begged.

Kady felt a laugh bubbling up in her throat. "Doesn't work that way. All right, one more big push. Just one more. And then it's over. Come on, Lucy, you can do this."

"No...I...can't. I...can't. I'm...too...tired."

"You're his mother," Byron said sternly, surprising them all. Up until now, he'd kept to the sidelines, completely quiet. "Are you going to fail him in his first few minutes of life?"

Lucy cursed him, but her anger gave her the strength she'd been missing. Panting, she ordered Juan to prop her up again. Closing her eyes tight, Lucy grunted and groaned. Her clenched knuckles were completely white as she pushed as hard as she could.

Kady maneuvered the shoulders out. The rest was easy. The small life slid into her hands.

"And we have a winner," Kady announced. "A beautiful baby boy."

"Boys ain't beautiful," Juan protested, but there was awe on his face, as if he couldn't believe that there was actually another living, breathing human being in the room with them.

"They are when they're little," Kady told him, pausing only for a second to look down at the brand-new baby in her hands. The next moment she was quickly clearing out his air passages. "His color's good."

"Sure, his color's good. He's mine, ain't he?" Juan boasted.

"Would you like to cut the cord?" Kady asked him, holding up the surgical scissors.

Juan turned a little green as he came closer. "Sure, why not? I'll cut the cord."

"Right here," Kady pointed out where. The next moment she was clamping down the end, right at the baby's belly button. She had a blanket ready and wrapped the infant in it. He was all but lost within the material, his small face peering out.

"This what all the fuss was about?" he murmured, more to the infant than to anyone within the crammed room.

"This was it." Struggling with all sorts of maternal feelings that were shifting through her, Kady raised her eyes to the young woman on the table. "You want to hold him?"

"He's mine, ain't he?" Lucy retorted, but with less bravado than she might have.

"No doubt about that." Gently Kady placed the baby in her arms and stepped back. She allowed the new parents to enjoy their child for a moment before she said, "You need to go to the hospital."

"Why?" Juan's head jerked up. "The kid's out." He looked down at the baby again, a little uncertainly this time. "They supposed to be this tiny?"

"He's a perfect size," Kady assured him. "But he and Lucy need to be checked out, to make sure everything's all right."

Juan scowled. "Can't you do that?"

She shook her head. "I don't have the necessary equipment here."

Leaving Lucy's side, Juan drew closer to Kady and lowered his voice. "Look, I ain't got the money—"

Kady held up her hand, cutting him off. She realized that he needed to save face in front of his new family. "Don't worry about it. We'll take you to Our Lady of Patience Memorial. They'll make some kind of arrangements." Or rather, she would, she added silently. There were provisions for cases such as these. They just required the right forms to be filled out, and someone to vouch for the patient. "Lucy and the baby need to go to the hospital," she repeated. "They need medical attention I can't give them." She turned to Byron. "We have to take them there."

Byron nodded. He'd already figured that out for himself. "Way ahead of you. I'll bring the car out around front."

"We'll take Lucy and the baby in Byron's car," she told Juan. "You can follow us in yours."

Juan looked at her suspiciously just as Byron opened the door. It was clear that he wasn't accustomed to having anyone go out of their way for him and was waiting for an ulterior motive to come through. "Why you doing all this for us?"

"Because I'm a doctor and it's what I'm supposed to do for my patients." She looked at Lucy. The teenager was looking at her baby with the beginning of motherly affection. "Do you have a name for him yet?" Lucy pressed her lips together and shook her head. Kady smiled reassuringly. "That's all right. Take your time picking one out. Pick out one you like saying. You're going to be using it a lot."

"Everything's all ready," Byron told her as he walked back into the exam room.

"All right, I'll take the baby," Kady said, gently lifting the small bundle from Lucy's arms. "I think you're going to have to carry Lucy to the car. You can't walk can you?" she asked Lucy. The teenager shook her head. She looked as weak as a day-old kitten.

"I'll take the baby," Juan corrected. "He's my son."

Kady offered no argument. Instead she carefully placed the newborn into his father's arms. There was love there, in his eyes, however faint.

"You're underpaid, you know that?" Bryon told her as they left Patience Memorial Hospital more than an hour later. Without thinking, he put his arm around her shoulders, shielding her from the wind. "Whatever the hell they're paying you, you're underpaid."

She was very aware of his arm, of him. Ever since she'd delivered the baby tonight, she felt as if all her senses were in a heightened state. "I don't get paid for the clinic," she reminded him. "I volunteer."

"In general," he clarified. She'd impressed him tonight, even more than she already had. She'd kept her cool under fire, looked down the barrel of a gun without flinching. Talked a punk into behaving. She was an extraordinary woman. "You keep hours that'd kill a truck driver."

"You keep them right along with me." For the past five days, he'd been with her every step of the way. More so because whenever she looked out into the living room in the middle of the night, he was up. As far as she could tell, Byron never slept. She at least got in a few hours here and there.

Byron shook his head. "This is just temporary," he said, referring to their arrangement. "What you do is permanent. When do you get to take it easy?" he wanted to know.

"When I'm dead," she joked.

"I believe that."

Byron unlocked the passenger door for her. Riding to the hospital, she'd been in the back with the baby and Lucy. "You hungry?"

"We could get some pizza to go," she suggested, remembering their first night together. She raised her voice so that he could hear as he rounded the hood. "You could get it with extra cheese—to celebrate."

He got in on the driver's side. Closing the door, he reached for his seat belt. "Celebrate?"

Her mouth curved. "Another new life coming into the world."

He thought about the disadvantages that baby probably had going against him. It wasn't going to be easy, growing up in that neighborhood and remaining on the straight and narrow, staying on the right side of the law.

But all that took a backseat to what he was feeling right now. He was still riding high on the wave of euphoria that he'd experienced. He'd never witnessed a baby being born before. Until it'd happened, he'd never given it much thought one way or another. But being there was like being front row center for a miracle. It was hard to remain cynical about it.

"That was pretty amazing, wasn't it?"

"What was?" She thought he was talking about Lucy giving birth, but she didn't want to jump to conclusions, didn't want to attribute her own responses to him. Didn't want, she realized, to be disappointed.

"Watching that new life struggling his way into the world. Didn't realize they were that tiny. Babies," he added.

"Some of them come larger, but that's the average size," she told him. He started up the car and they made their way out of the lot. "Sasha's delivered babies half that size."

"Half?" he echoed. It seemed incredible to him. "How do they survive?"

They wouldn't have, fifty years ago, she thought. "Through the wonders of modern medicine and technology." She leaned back in the passenger seat, closing her eyes and stretching her body. Everything felt as if it was aching. "Man, I'm so tired."

He stole a glance at her as he eased to a stop at the light. Her back was arched and her breasts were slightly raised. For a second he forgot all about her being a doctor. His mind was on the woman beside him.

Byron forced his eyes back on the road. His hands were gripping the wheel a little tighter than he would have liked. He drew in a breath slowly, subtly. "Didn't think you got tired."

She opened her eyes again and looked at him, a smile playing on her lips. She was glad he was at the clinic today. It helped, just knowing he was there. "Then you haven't been paying attention."

That was just the trouble, Byron thought. He was paying attention to her. Way too much attention. And that, he knew, was ultimately going to interfere with his job.

He thought it best to change the conversation. "You always that fearless?"

She laughed at the thought. "I was scared the whole time."

"What?" She certainly hadn't looked as if she was afraid. "You're pulling my leg."

She tried not to think about touching any part of his anatomy, leg or anything else. "No, I'm not. I was scared that I'd do something wrong. I've only assisted at a birth once, and that felt like it was a hundred years ago."

"No, I meant with the gangbanger."

She hadn't thought about being afraid of Juan. Things had happened too quickly. And she had gotten good at reading people's faces. They *had* to act tough in that neighborhood.

"He wasn't going to hurt us. He was more scared than Lucy was."

She was a little too confident for her own good, Byron thought. It would get her into trouble someday when he wasn't there to cover her back. "In my experience, scared and guns are a bad combination."

She turned in her seat to look at him. Her smile was so warm, he could almost feel it. "Then I guess I was lucky to have you with me."

"Yeah, lucky," he grunted. He didn't trust himself to say what other thoughts were running through his head.

Chapter 12

Taking the keys to her apartment from Kady, Byron gave her the pizza box to hold, then unlocked the door. Instead of a well-lit apartment, there was only a single light on next to the door. With Tania still away, she would have thought that Natalya would have had every light on.

"Nat, we're home," Kady called out. There was no response of any kind. "Nat, are you home?"

She began to walk in, only to have her access barred. Kady looked at Byron. He shook his head. The man was just too cautious and melodramatic.

Putting his finger to his lips, he motioned for her to stand right inside the doorway. She knew he intended to check out the other rooms, just as had become his habit. This was fine when she had a drop of energy to her name, but she was too tired tonight for this. All she wanted to do was grab a few bites and then fall straight into bed.

Resigned, Kady watched as he moved from the living room to the rooms beyond, his handgun drawn, his attention razor sharp.

Byron swept through the apartment quickly, efficiently, checking into the closets, into every conceivable hiding place. There was no one lying in wait. As he made his way through the kitchen and back into the living room, he holstered his weapon.

"You sister's gone for the night. She's spending it at Mike's."

Kady stared at him. Was he into mind reading now? "How do you know that?"

He nodded toward the kitchen. "She left you a note on the refrigerator."

Kady looked down at the box in her hands, shifting her hold on it. "I guess then it's just you, me and the pizza."

"Guess so," he agreed. Even as he said it, the apartment began to feel smaller. More intimate. Way too intimate.

Turning around, he crossed back to the living room and began to turn on more lights. Byron worked his way into the hall, then the kitchen.

Stunned, Kady watched him. "What are you

doing?" she finally asked, following him into the kitchen.

"Turning on the lights."

"I can see that." Setting the pizza box on the kitchen table, Kady deliberately turned on her heel and made the rounds, turning off the lights he'd just turned on. When he looked at her quizzically, she said, "Don't you know there's an energy crisis on? Besides," she said, returning to the kitchen and crossing back to the table, "I don't need all that light." She smiled up into his face. "I have you."

He closed the distance between them. When he spoke, it felt as if there was a layer of cotton on his tongue and the roof of his mouth. "Last time I checked, I didn't glow in the dark."

"No," she replied, the smile continuing to play on her lips, "you don't. But you'll protect me from what's in the dark."

Damn, if he took so much as a breath, he'd be brushing up against her. How could one small woman unnerve him like this? She was too close. Much too close.

Much too desirable.

He tried to get a grip. "How about if what's in the dark is me?"

Kady could have sworn she felt his breath on her face, on her skin. Her pulse began to accelerate as anticipation took hold. Things were happening inside of her, things she couldn't stop. It was as if someone had thrown a switch. Or taken off her blinders.

Her breath backed up into her lungs. The words came out in a whisper. "I don't need protecting from you."

Unable to help himself, he ran his thumb along her lower lip. "I wouldn't be too sure of that."

Every part of his body was throbbing, urging him on. Urging him to lower his head and kiss her now, before the moment was lost; before he came to his senses; before he remembered that he was a professional and she was his assignment, albeit assigned by him.

Self-assigned or not, that still didn't mean that he was allowed to take advantage of the situation—or of her.

Kady's knees felt shaky. "Are you going to kiss me?"

Byron made one last-ditch effort to pull himself free of the quicksand he'd ventured into. "I was thinking of the pizza."

"You can kiss the pizza later. Kiss me now." And then, to ensure that he wouldn't pull away, Kady rose on her toes, bringing her mouth even closer to his. Less than a breath away.

Unable to resist, Byron framed her face with his hands and kissed her.

He'd meant only to indulge himself a little, to bring an end to the conversation and move on. He and Kady were both hungry, after all, and the pizza was right there, waiting.

He was hungry for a lot more than pizza, he realized the moment he made contact with her mouth; the moment things went shooting off in his veins, creating a light show in his head. Damn near pulling him into a swirling vortex.

Drawing his head back, Byron struggled to focus as he looked at her. He was more than a little stunned. There was power in that kiss. Power and feeling. And so much more he couldn't even begin to identify it.

"Wow," he thought.

It wasn't until she murmured, "Yes, 'wow,'" that he realized he's said the word out loud. Embarrassment tugged at him, but not for long.

The next moment she was kissing him. And he lost any and all ability to resist. His control was usurped by desire, hot and heavy. And demanding.

Since his divorce, the women who had drifted in and out of his life had left no impression on Byron's soul. They were there for a night, to satisfy something that was purely physical. It was all just a matter of supply and demand.

He realized that it wasn't just his hands he was filling up, it was the emptiness. For some reason she made it fade, made it disappear. She filled the space with her essence. Her presence.

He'd never felt this kind of desire before, this

kind of urgency, to take, to savor, to feel. But this thing—whatever this thing was—was racing far too quickly through him, shaking foundations, breaking down fences.

Byron told himself that he was moving too fast. The last thing he wanted was to overwhelm her. He was her bodyguard, not her predator.

With effort Byron drew his head back. "Look, I'm not sure what's going on here—"

"I've got a book that explains it all," she told him breathlessly, never taking her hands away from him. "We'll look at it later."

He was trying to stop this for her own good, but he was having trouble stringing together coherent words when she was touching him like that.

"But—"

"Byron," she breathed, wrapping her arms around his neck. "You talk too much."

A hint of a smile curved his mouth as Byron shook his head in wonder. "First time anyone's ever said that to me."

Any reply she might have rendered evaporated as he brought his mouth down to hers.

Kady lost herself in the sensation he was creating throughout her body, in the taste of him. Her mind was swirling and sending everything out of focus.

She hadn't realized, until this moment, as she let her instincts take over, how much she missed being with a man. Cynthia Applegate's dying despite all her best efforts had shut something down inside of her.

But there were parts of her that did not thrive well under enforced denial. And while she'd never just gone from man to man with no regard but the pursuit of pleasure, she'd had a healthy love life in only the most cursory sense. For Kady love had never run deep, had never gone down to anything beyond the very first surface layer. She didn't let it. Before that young mother's death had redefined her world, she'd loved being part of a pair—until things became serious or the first sign of discord arose. Once that happened, she'd move on—quickly— until she found someone new to couple up with.

But after Cynthia's death, she'd lost all desire to be part of anything outside of her initial foundations.

Until this man had come into her life.

This man who insisted on keeping her safe, on looking over her shoulder to make sure there was no one around to hurt her. Not because she'd asked him to but because some code of ethics, of honor, made him. In a very odd way Byron reminded her of her father. Minus the unique language syntax.

Now there was only this flaming need burning her up inside. A need to be held, to be made love to.

His hands were swift, gentle, and he was melting her as he let them glide over her body. Over her.

Byron couldn't help himself. Even though a part of him fairly shouted that this was all wrong, that he should stop, he couldn't seem to put the brakes on. Desire outweighed good sense almost from the first moment they'd walked into the apartment. Certainly from the moment he realized that they were alone together.

More than looks, more than a mouth that drove him to distraction, he responded to her integrity. To someone who was a doer rather than someone who let life take them from place to place, from moment to moment.

Watching Kady earlier at the clinic, unintimidated by the people she tended, moving forcefully as she did what she had to do, he found himself moved with admiration. If he could love, if he could actually feel something, it would be for a woman like Kady.

An urgency propelled him, pushing him on. Making him take what he wouldn't have even felt worthy of asking for.

He couldn't remember ever wanting this much, ever being taken prisoner by the desires, the passions that were even now shaking up the very foundations of his being. Couldn't remember anything clearly.

Only her.

His hands moved quickly over Kady's body, caressing, undressing, doing away with the barriers that impeded what he knew in his bones had to be. Feeling her fingers fly over his torso, making short work of his own clothing, only added to the intensity of the desire that was growing in his veins. In his very body.

Over and over again, Byron kissed her, feeling as if he's never be able to sate his need. Over and over again, like waves venturing farther and farther up the shore, desire filled him. Relentlessly. Taking his breath away. Filling his head just as she seemed to fill the rest of him. Making the loneliness retreat into the shadows.

He dove his fingers into her hair and brought her closer to him. His mouth traveled from her lips to her neck, to her breasts. To every part of her. And still he couldn't seem to get enough. Still he needed more.

Lovemaking had always been equal before, Kady thought. If anything, she'd been the one who led. But not with Byron.

With Byron, all she could feel was that she was on a wild journey, riding the crest of a hurricane like some imaginary cartoon character. Holding on for dear life.

There was no give and take, no opportunity to give at all, only take. She was completely on the receiving end. And so deliriously happy she couldn't even begin to put it into words. He made her body sing. And want him so badly with every fiber of her being that Kady didn't think she would be able to stand it for very much longer.

With his mouth, his hands, his very breath, he brought her to the absolute peak of sensation, causing shivers through her body. Leaving it vibrating with pleasure.

And wanting more.

Waiting for more.

Once, twice, three times, her body arched, absorbing the explosions that he created within her until she was spent and panting on the sofa.

She was so exhausted she could hardly muster the energy to breathe.

Byron couldn't hold back any longer. He'd done what he could, giving her a small measure of the pleasure that being with her created within him. But a man could only hold back so long.

He was no longer a self-contained tower of strength the way he'd once believed himself to be. He was just a man. A man with needs.

His mouth covered hers as Byron repositioned himself over her, slowly bringing his body down on hers. He felt her shifting urgently beneath him. Rising to meet him halfway. He felt the sizzle between their bodies.

Then, drawing his head back so that he could look at her, at her eyes, her face, Byron sheathed himself in her. When she moaned, the sound filled with anticipation, with pleasure, he began to move more quickly. She caught him by surprise, wrapping her legs around him. Sealing herself to him as closely as he had sealed himself to her.

The tempo increased as the fire in his belly, in his loins, heightened, demanding release. Even so, joined to her this way, Byron did his best to continue. To hold back for as long as he could.

But it was out of his hands, out of his control.

He drove himself into her farther and farther, until he felt her arching up against him, crying out words he didn't understand. Words that nevertheless, because of the feeling throbbing around each syllable, drove him over the brink.

Kady's fingertips dug into his skin as they experienced the final moment, the final explosion, together.

Breathing heavily, Byron gathered Kady to him. Holding her as tightly as he was physically able. Not wanting to let go of the moment. His heart was slamming against his chest. Against her.

Byron could feel her heart stop pounding quite so hard, could feel the rhythm gradually slowing until it was close to normal.

Taking a deep breath, he withdrew. In the limited space afford by the sofa, he claimed a place beside her, one arm still beneath her head.

Kady nestled into it. In a moment she'd feel the chill beginning, feel the lack of his warmth mingling with hers. But right now she could still feel the impression of his skin on hers and she savored it.

"Am I glad you didn't charge me for being my bodyguard. I don't think I could have afforded that, just now."

Byron turned his head to look at her, trying to determine if she was kidding. She'd uttered her words so seriously that for a moment he thought she meant them. But then he thought he detected a glimmer of a smile in the corner of her mouth.

A sense of humor was something he was going to have to work on, he thought.

"That's not part of the package," he informed her.

She tried hard to suppress a grin, then gave up.

Byron propped himself up on his elbow, looking down at her. He felt desire beginning to blossom again and was astonished at the realization. What kind of spell had she cast over him? He didn't begin to understand it or himself right now. This wasn't like him.

Kady felt as if she'd just finished running a marathon. And the damn thing was, she wanted to put her running shoes on again. "I'm the first person I know who's had an out-of-body experience." That's what it had felt like, she thought, as if she'd left her body and hovered above it, watching wonderful things happen and feeling them by proxy.

Shifting on the sofa, Kady turned her body into his. A tingling sensation began to dance all through her. The tempo began to pick up again as anticipation took hold. She could only marvel at the effect he had on her. "Where did you learn to do that?"

He brushed her hair from her face. "Haven't a clue."

The smile began in her eyes and spread, taking in her lips and then all of her until she seemed to radiate with it. "Do it again."

He didn't smile often. But when he did, she caught herself thinking that it was damn near lethal. She felt her heart lurch.

"Give me a minute."

In response, she raised her right wrist and stared at her watch. "Okay."

The last thing she remembered hearing, before the world slipped back into flames, was his laugh.

Chapter 13

The phone rang, splintering the silence, jarring them both out of the sound sleep that came after intense lovemaking.

Trying to focus and pull herself into the moment, Kady groped for the phone as her other hand searched for the light switch. She secured both at the same time.

The numbers she was staring at registered. It was barely three o'clock. Kady groaned inwardly.

Beside her, she felt Byron stirring. The next moment he'd sat bolt upright, his body tense, ready. She felt him turn in her direction, obviously waiting to discover who was on the other end of the line. Did he forget she was a cardiologist?

"Dr. Pulaski." Kady pressed her lips together, stifling the yawn that immediately came on the heels of her declaration. They'd gotten less than three hours sleep. She had a feeling she wasn't getting any more.

"Is this Dr. Leokadia Pulaski?" the young female voice on the other end of the land line asked uncertainly.

Kady dragged a hand through her hair, hoping she didn't look like a hurricane had tossed her aside. "Last time I checked."

The voice immediately went from uncertain to apologetic. "I'm sorry to bother you, Dr. Pulaski, but one of your patients was brought in by the paramedics a little while ago with chest pains. A Mr. Jack Everly. He's been asking for you."

The name conjured up an image of a short, heavyset man with a wealth of white hair and a face that could have passed for Santa Claus. The man was close to eighty.

Kady sat up. If Jack Everly had arrived at Patience Memorial by ambulance, the least she could do was check on him, she thought, resigned to putting any further communion with her pillow on hold.

Taking a deep breath, she told the woman who called, "I'll be right there," and hung up.

"Be right where?" Byron wanted to know.

Turning to look at him, Kady was struck again

by the same feeling that had ultimately brought her to this place in time: in bed beside her self-appointed bodyguard. Naked from the waist up, the blanket loosely tucked around his lower torso, he brought to mind why there was a need for such words as *magnificent.* God knew he was enough to render the average woman speechless. And very grateful.

It took her a second to find her voice and bank down the fresh volley of desire that had exploded in her veins.

"At the hospital," she told him. "One of my patients was just brought in by ambulance."

A sigh escaped his lips as Byron scrubbed his hand over his face. He was doing his best not to dwell on the fact that she was completely nude under the blanket that was outlining her body.

"There enough time for a shower?" he wanted to know.

"For you." She threw aside the blanket and got out of bed. She hurried over to the bureau, aware that he was watching her. It took some of the chill out of the air. "I have to go right down."

Kady took out a matching lingerie set, then hurried into a pair of jeans and a light-gray pullover. Grabbing a clip from the top of the bureau, she pulled back her hair and fastened it at her nape.

There'd be no shower for him, either. "Where you go, I go," he reminded her.

Rising from the bed, he pulled the blanket off and wound it around the lower half of his torso like an oversize bath towel. He held it in place against his waist as he went back to the living room to retrieve the clothes she'd pulled off his body last night.

Modest. She wouldn't have thought it, Kady mused. But then again, maybe she should have. There was something touchingly old-fashioned about her bodyguard. But when it came to lovemaking, he was definitely very state-of-the-art.

She passed him as she went to the kitchen, sparing only one glance in his direction.

Kady rummaged through the refrigerator, tossing a couple of slices of raisin bread and two apples into a sandwich bag.

Breakfast for two, she thought as she crossed to the front door. Byron was already there, dressed and ready to go. Looking as if nothing out of the ordinary had happened between them.

But it had. Something very out of the ordinary had happened between them last night, and right now she hadn't a clue how to handle it.

Emerging out of the silence he'd maintained all the way down in the elevator, he turned to her as they got out on the ground floor of the building's parking garage. "I just want you to know that last night wasn't supposed to happen."

She did what she could to roll with the punch,

telling herself that there was a myriad of reasons why he might have said that. Fear of commitment being the front runner. He needn't have worried, she thought. She suffered from the same malady.

But she kept that to herself for the time being. "Not on your schedule of things to do, huh?"

He gathered from her smile that for some reason she thought he was joking. "I'm serious."

She spotted his car and picked up her pace. "Yes, you are and you should stop." She glanced at him as they reached his vehicle. "Lighten up, Byron. This is the twenty-first century. People sleep with other people all the time—although not much 'sleeping' was involved with us." She grinned. He didn't respond in kind. This was more serious than she thought. The man needed reassurance. "Don't worry, Byron. I'm not about to stand on some roof-top, announcing our engagement." The last word triggered a recent memory. There was a message on her answering machine from Thursday afternoon that she hadn't bothered to respond to yet. Not that she really needed to. It was assumed that her answer was going to be yes.

She'd put off mentioning the message because she'd hoped to slip away on her own to attend. But after last night, Kady realized that she didn't want to attend the party alone. She wanted him there with her, even if, as she'd just pointed out, it didn't actually mean anything.

"Speaking of which," she did her best to sound casual, "my parents are throwing Natalya and Mike an engagement party next week. It's on Saturday. Six o'clock. Give or take half an hour." Her mother was *never* ready on time, her father made it a point to always be early. They split the difference.

Pressing the remote, he unlocked the car. Byron pocketed the device before opening her door. There was more than a hint of suspicion and confusion on his face. "Why are you telling me this?"

Kady slid into the passenger seat. The leather felt cold even through her jeans and sweater. "So that you can pencil it in."

"Thanks," he told her, getting in on his side, "but there's no reason to 'pencil' it in. I'm not going." He steered clear of things like weddings and engagement parties. Anything that involved a wealth of relatives. He had no desire to be absorbed by anyone's family, certainly not hers.

She feigned surprise as she looked at him. "What happened to 'where you go, I go'?"

Byron blew out a breath. He'd forgotten for a moment. Of course he had to go with her. The first principle of being a bodyguard was to keep guarding the body.

He set his jaw hard, far from happy about the prospect of what loomed ahead. He'd rather sit twelve hours in a car on a stakeout than spend two hours watching people mingling at a party, button-holing him and bombarding him with either advice or questions. "What time did you say it was?"

"Six. Give or take," she added, then grinned as he gunned the engine a bit louder than she thought was necessary. "Don't worry, I'll protect you from my mother."

He peeled out of the parking garage smoothly. There were no other cars around to get in his way. "Excuse me?"

"I'll protect you from my mother," she repeated. She might as well prepare him now. "Mama tends to come on strong."

The light on the next block turned red before he had the opportunity to shoot through the intersection. Putting his foot on the brake, he looked at her significantly. "Must run in the family."

Rather than take offense, Kady merely laughed.

The melodic sound filled up the space within the darkened car.

"And this is?"

Asking the question as she pulled open the front door, Magda Pulaski looked like a composite older version of her daughters. All the Pulaski sisters were present at the engagement party that was being thrown in the older couple's Queens home. Even Tania had flown in for the occasion, juggling a tight schedule that required her to fly back late Sunday evening in order to continue with the hospital's exchange program on Monday morning.

But right now, Magda was not focusing on her traveling daughter, or even the daughter for whom she and Josef had thrown this party. She was looking at the tall, serious-looking young man standing just behind Kady. As if he was using his body to shield her from the wind. And everything else.

Who was this man who had come into Kady's life? Because, if she was any judge of the matter, her daughter was different tonight. Far more like her old self. It only took one look to see that.

"Her bodyguard," Josef announced, coming up behind his wife to join them in the doorway. He smiled proudly when Kady looked at him in surprise. "Did not think that I would know, yes?" He shifted the glass of vodka from one hand to the other in order to thump his chest with his right hand. "But I am knowing everything."

Kady laughed. She should have realized that, with his contacts on both the force and via the security firm he now worked for with his old partner, her father would have found out about Byron. "Bryon, I'd like you to meet my father, superdad."

Josef scowled, or pretended to, as he glanced at his daughter, simultaneously putting his hand out. "Kady is making a joke. No respect, these young girls. Josef Pulaski," he introduced himself with a smart nod of his head.

"Byron." He paused a moment, then added his last name as he caught Kady's eye. "Kennedy."

Still holding his hand, Josef shook it harder. "Please to meeting you, Byron Kennedy." Releasing the man's hand, he placed his arm around his wife's shoulders. "This is my lovely wife, Magda."

"And this is your frozen daughter, Kady," Kady interrupted. "Can we please get off the porch and into the house? It's cold out here."

Josef elaborately stepped out of the way, gesturing into the house. He looked back at Byron, who followed Kady in. "I am not envying you, guarding this one. If you are needing help, Byron, you have only to be asking."

Kady glanced around. It looked as if they were the last ones here. The house was jammed with people. Just the way her parents liked it. "That's Dad's subtle way of saying he wants to take over," she told Byron.

Not to be left out, Magda, who had been shrewdly assessing this new face from the sidelines, now moved front and center. Coming between Kady and Byron, Magda laced her arm through his.

"So, Mr. Byron Kennedy, tell me about yourself. What is it you are doing when you are not forced to listen to this one?" She indicated Kady just in case there was any doubt who she was referring to.

Kady rolled her eyes. This was fast, even for her mother. "Mama, let the man get a drink or two under his belt before you start pumping him."

"I am not pumping," Magda protested with feeling. "I am talking. Making conversation." Of her two parents, it was her mother who had better command of the language, although none of them had ever said as much to their father. He had an ego that they were careful not to bruise. "And so is Byron," Magda concluded, smiling broadly at the man she had trapped against her side.

"Unleash him, Mama," Kady said. Then, in case her mother didn't understand, Kady drew her mother's arm away from Byron's.

Magda protested, just as Kady knew she would.

Byron had a feeling, as he listened to the exchange between mother and daughter, that he had suddenly gotten in too deep. He thought about Kady's comment about alcoholic reinforcement. Although he never drank on the job anymore, right about now a drink was beginning to sound pretty good to him.

As if reading his mind, a tall, slim man with hair the color of midnight and friendly eyes approached him. He was holding two chunky glasses half-filled with an amber liquid and held one out to him.

"Tony Santini," the man introduced himself. "Sasha's husband," he added, although it was obvious that the woman's name meant nothing to

Byron. "The pretty one over there." Using his drink, he pointed out a dark-haired woman talking to several other people.

Byron took the information in. "Thanks." Turning away from Kady and her parents, he shifted toward Tony as he wrapped his hand around the wide glass. His expression was somewhat wary.

"Don't worry, they're harmless," Tony assured him. He paused to take a sip of his drink. "Overwhelming, but harmless. No sense in fighting it," he advised. "They're good people and you'll get used to them."

Byron shook his head. There was no need for the advice. He doubted very much that he'd be around for that much longer.

"Don't have to. I'm only going to be around until the trial's over." He assumed that, like the old man, Kady's brother-in-law knew all about Kady's part in the upcoming trial.

He could have sworn he heard Tony murmur something like, "Famous last words," under his breath before he took another long sip of his own drink, but he wasn't quite sure.

"So, I am hearing that you were on the police force once," Josef said, materializing at his side. "We are having this in common." Laying one hand on Byron's shoulder, he looked over at his son-in-law. "Tony is a detective. I served also," he went on, then punctuated his statement with a quick sip of his blood-warming vodka. "Twenty-eight years," he continued. "So, tell me…" Anyone familiar with Josef knew he was at the beginning of launching into a long question and an even longer narrative. Gently the older man started to lead him away from Tony and everyone else.

A feeling of uncertainty had Byron looking over his shoulder toward Kady. But she was still verbally feinting and parrying with her mother. Byron's gut told him that he was getting the better of the deal.

He did his best to remain on the outskirts. It had never been difficult for him before. His quiet, with-drawn manner was enough to send people seeking conversation and companionship elsewhere.

But the Pulaskis and their friends, he quickly learned, were those legendary horses of a different color. A loving, outgoing bunch of people, they had absolutely no concept of what it meant to leave someone alone. And they didn't. He was pulled into one conversation after another, his opinion sought and cohered. If he intended to keep his own counsel, he never got the chance. They assaulted him with their vitality, their curiosity, their warmth. In short order, he found himself becoming, if not one of them, at least part of them. Resistance, he came to realize, was futile.

* * *

"It is time to be toasting the happy couple," Magda announced, raising her voice after the seven-course meal had rendered everyone but the heartiest immobile.

Magda raised her glass as well, looking toward Natalya and Mike, seated at the far end of the last table, a princess and her prince. Magda beamed at them, endless affection emanating from every word.

"May you always be as happy as your father and I are."

Josef rose to stand beside his wife. He mugged for the crowd. "Again, she is taking the words from my mouth. But after all these years, I am being used to it." As if to prove it, Josef kissed his wife's forehead before raising his own glass high. He looked at his second daughter and the man she'd chosen to face forever with. "Natalya, Michael, what she is saying—double. *Na zdrowia*." Uttering the Polish words, which roughly translated meant "to your health," he threw back the clear liquid, downing it as if it was a glass of water.

"Um." Sasha cleared her throat. All eyes turned toward her and her husband. A pink hue graced her cheeks. "Since we're making announcements…" she began almost shyly.

Of the sisters, she was the most soft-spoken one, the one who craved the least attention. But, as the oldest, she also knew her place in the scheme of things, and this was something that her mother and father were going to want to hear as soon as possible. Given that she loved all of them equally, she and Tony had decided that making a mass announcement was the best way to go. If they called them one by one, someone would be insulted about being the last to be notified. And if her mother wasn't first, Sasha knew she would never hear the end of it.

Sasha needn't have agonized over her choice of words, or the fact that her timing might take away from the attention Natalya and Mike deserved. Her mere attempt to make the announcement was all that her mother needed.

Magda was immediately alert. The next moment she was making her way over to Sasha and Tony, exclaiming things that only a handful of people understood. She grabbed Sasha and Tony each by the hand, then simply threw her arms around them, hugging them both. There were tears in her eyes.

"A baby," she cried when she finally released them. "You are having a baby!"

Sasha looked at Tony. Magda always seemed to be one step ahead. "Did I tell you that my mother was also part fortune teller? And, yes, Mama, Tony and I are having a baby."

Magda wiped away the tears that insisted on spilling out. "When?"

Sasha exchanged glances with her husband. They'd only found out a few days ago. "In the summer." She looked at her mother. "It's going to be an August baby, actually."

Magda clapped her hands together. She looked as if she was ready to dance around the room, Kady thought, watching her mother.

"An August baby." And then she turned to look at Natalya and Mike. "And another wedding. Two of my girls married and one to be a mother." No one listening to her doubted that she felt as if her prayers had been answered. At least some of them.

"What more can a mother be wishing for, eh?" Josef chuckled, joining her. He slipped his arm around her shoulders, his own eyes shining.

"Well," Magda said slowly, "I can think of a few things." To make her point, Magda looked over toward where Kady and Byron were seated. Her long gaze took in not just them but Tania and Marja as well.

Kady spoke for all of them as she shook her head. "Mama, you are just never satisfied, are you?"

Magda looked at her knowingly, a smile blooming on her lips.

"Oh, but I will be, Kady," Magda assured her. "I will be."

Kady immediately looked at Byron, half expecting him to be making a beeline for the front door. But he was still in his seat, albeit a little uncomfortably. Their eyes met.

She leaned over toward him. "I'm sorry. You're

going to have to forgive my mother, but most mothers act this way."

"I wouldn't know. Mine died a long time ago," he reminded her.

She remembered. Remembered everything he'd ever told her. It should have made her uneasy. But it didn't.

"Don't say that too loudly," she warned, "or my mother will adopt you."

He had a feeling that she wasn't really kidding.

Chapter 14

As the trial date grew closer, Byron was growing edgier.

The closer the start of the trial came, the more certain he felt that Kady was in danger. And the closer the trail came, the closer it was to being over. Which meant that he was that much closer to going back to a life that didn't include a sparkly, vibrant cardiologist. A woman who, quite frankly, knocked out all the underpinnings that had kept his life on the stable, narrow path that he had gotten accustomed to.

When he'd first offered his services, he'd come to Kady not really wanting to get involved, but knowing that he had to do so on a cursory level. As cursory as possible. He owed it to Milos Plageanos, just as he owed to him the fact that he was still among the living.

But despite the strictest promises to himself, Byron had to admit that he had gotten involved far deeper than he'd ever intended or actually owed to his late employer.

While he still told himself that he wanted no strings, Byron wasn't quite as convinced of that as he'd once been. Being around Kady 24/7 had unlocked doors within him. Had stirred feelings in places he could have sworn no longer had feelings. If he were being completely honest, he would have to admit that there was something about this woman that made him feel alive. Alive for the first time in years.

It'd been two weeks since he had found himself pressed into attending her sister's engagement party with her. Two weeks since his ramparts had been breached by a warm Polish family that couldn't seem to take no for an answer and most definitely did take prisoners.

And three weeks since the first time he'd made love with her. The first time, but not last.

He made love with her every night.

The first night, he knocked on her bedroom door after everyone was asleep. He'd debated a full half hour with himself before finally giving in to the relentless desire that was giving him no peace. The door to Kady's bedroom had flown open and he had all but unceremoniously been pulled inside the room.

"I thought you'd never come," Kady had said, shutting the door behind him and leaning against it in case he changed his mind about spending the night with her.

He remembered looking at her, surprised and just a bit confused. She had that effect on him. "You *knew* I was going to come in?"

Her smile was nothing short of radiant as she nodded. "Pretty much." And then she'd raised her eyes to his, melting most of his internal structure. "So, are you going to kiss me or are you going to force me to jump your bones?"

Byron found himself smiling as well, something he wasn't really accustomed to. But she made him want to smile.

"The first," he chose, taking her into his arms.

"Good." She'd snuggled up against him. "Because I hate being pushy."

She had a way of mingling wickedness with innocence. "Too late," he told her just before he brought his lips to hers. And sank into a paradise of his own making.

Each night as he approached her door, it became a little easier. A little easier surrendering a bit of himself. Because each time, there was a new adventure waiting for him. That was what their lovemaking was, an adventure. New and different, yet somehow, still steadfastly the same.

He couldn't explain it any better than that. Because somehow, while the location and the woman remained the same, Kady still managed to bring a fresh excitement to their lovemaking. The air fairly sizzled between them from the moment he entered the room until the moment they fell asleep, spent beyond words. Try as he might, Byron couldn't remember *ever* being this alive.

But all of this, the lovemaking, the reason for his even being in her life, was going to end the moment the trial did.

He told himself that it was a good thing. That he couldn't continue this kind of existence indefinitely. For one thing, he was going to have to seek a position that paid him. Although he had no desperate need for money at the moment, thanks to the generous bequest Milos had given him, eventually he needed to plan for the future.

Something he hadn't done since before Bobby was killed.

And the approaching trial was a good thing for another reason as well. Because once the trial ended, so would his excuse. There'd be no reason to be in her life anymore, to hover about like a wingless guardian angel. There'd be no reason to shadow her to the hospital, or stand around at the free clinic. He'd be free.

The thought should have heartened him.

It didn't.

"You know," Kady said early one morning in the kitchen as she got ready to leave for the hospital, "this might all be just paranoia on your part." She was referring to the lecture he'd just given her—that she took too many chances going to the clinic. They argued about it every Friday, and sometimes before. She would have thought he'd have given up by now.

Byron set down the newspaper he was only marginally perusing. The furrow on his forehead deepened. "Paranoia?"

"That Skourous's grandson is going to try to kill me to make sure I don't testify against him at the trial."

"He's got nothing to lose and everything to gain by getting rid of you," Byron told her, not for the first time. "A third murder wouldn't faze him."

"It's been a month now," she pointed out, "and nothing's happened."

He folded the paper without looking at it. His eyes held hers. "Doesn't mean it's not going to."

Kady shook her head, but her tone was affectionate. Though she'd tried hard not to get involved, she found herself caring a great deal for this man. "Ever the pessimist."

"Better a live pessimist than a dead optimist," he countered.

He had her there, she supposed. Leaning over

him at the table, Kady ran the back of her hand along his cheek. Vivid memories of last night crowded in her head. He'd managed to set her world on fire even more so than usual. What was she going to do once he was gone? How was she going to manage?

A smile hovered on her lips. "Can't argue about the live part," Kady murmured.

She went to caress him again, but he caught her wrist. His eyes darted toward the doorway, silently communicating the arrival of one of her sisters.

Grinning, Tania pretended to shield her eyes with her hand as she continued walking toward the refrigerator. Tania couldn't function in the morning until she had a glass of orange juice in her veins.

"I see nothing," she announced cheerfully. "Carry on." A stifled giggle followed in the wake of the last two words. "Oops, sorry," she murmured.

Crossing to the cupboard, the slender brunette took out a bowl for her cereal. Tania had a huge affinity for cereals that came in multicolors and loudly proclaimed the favorite cartoon character of the moment on its boxes.

Kady glanced at the box and shook her head. "You really should try eating something more nutritious, Tania. You're a doctor, you should know better."

The look on Tania's face was sheer innocence. "Feeds the inner kid in me," she told her sister in between bites.

Kady shrugged, temporarily surrendering. "You are what you eat."

Tania looked down at the bowl of multicolored circles bobbing up and down in a sea of milk that was quickly turning into a rainbow of colors. "I can live with that."

"Following that logic," Byron commented, his voice resuming its laidback tone, "that makes me a cup of coffee."

Kady stopped and very deliberately looked down into his mug, studying it. "Strong, dark and rich." She raised her eyes to his, doing her best to deadpan. "I'd say that just about covers it."

He ignored the other words and only caught the one that was glaringly wrong. "Rich?"

"Inside," Kady told him. He was still sitting down. Standing over him, she slipped her hand in the space created between the buttons of his shirt. Her fingertips tapped his chest. "In here." Her eyes took him prisoner. "Where it counts."

Very deliberately he removed her hand, even though part of him wanted to leave it there. "Just proves you don't know me at all."

Kady cocked her head. "Maybe I do and you don't," she countered. And then she glanced at her watch. Traffic had better be accommodating today. Even though she lived fairly close to the hospital, it was easy to be late if the traffic gods were against you.

She picked up her purse from the floor beside the chair she'd vacated. "C'mon if you're coming. I don't like being late."

No, he thought, rising and pushing in his chair, she liked being early. Which suited him just fine.

Everything about the woman, he thought darkly, suited him just fine. Which was why he couldn't wait until this trial was behind them. He was getting too accustomed to her. Too accustomed to spending all of his time with her, to slipping into her bed at night. Too accustomed to waking up in the morning and feeling her warm flesh right there next to his. It was getting out of hand.

That route only led to disappointment. And lack of control over his own life. He did better on his own.

Or so he told himself as he led the way out of the apartment.

"You know, it's such a lovely evening, why don't we walk home tonight?" Kady asked. It was a full ten hours later and she was finally getting ready to leave. Slipping on her coat, she'd glanced out the window at the darkened skyline. The crisp, clear night had prompted the impulsive suggestion.

How could she be so intelligent and yet so naive? "Because we drove here and I need the car," he told her patiently. Bryon put his jacket on. "And because you'd be exposed."

For once she wanted to pretend that they were

just another couple, not a bodyguard and his charge. "You'd be there to protect me," she protested, knowing that the battle was already lost. But she wouldn't have been her mother's daughter if she gave up so easily.

"In case you haven't noticed, I'm not bullet-proof," Byron informed her tersely.

With a slight frown, Kady lifted her shoulders and let them fall again. Pick your battles, her mother had always counseled. And she didn't feel like fighting tonight. She just wanted to enjoy the evening with him.

"Okay, the car it is."

Leaving last-minute instructions regarding three patients with the young woman at the nurses' station, Kady turned and fell into step beside Byron.

The elevator was waiting for them when they reached the far end of the floor. Pressing the lowest button on the pad, they took the car down into the bottom level of the parking garage.

Today had been an exceptionally busy day and the parking garage reflected the traffic within the hospital. When they'd arrived this morning, it had taken Byron almost twenty minutes, going from one level to another, to find an empty space.

In contrast, the level was half-empty when they got off the elevator.

Walking beside her, keeping his body between Kady and any vehicles that might be coming or going, Byron made sure that she neither got ahead of him nor fell behind. The back of his neck prickled tonight, making him uneasy. It was probably nothing, but then again, he had learned to trust his gut.

Maybe he was becoming paranoid, the way she'd said.

He knew she'd been serious about wanting to walk outside. Byron turned toward her to say something along the lines that maybe, once the trial was behind her, they could go for that walk.

But he never got the opportunity.

The sound of tires squealing penetrated the stillness. The next moment a black sedan came barreling down on them out of nowhere. Tinted windows prevented seeing in to make even the vaguest identification of who was behind the wheel.

The vehicle looked as if it was coming straight at them, the driver intent on mowing them down. Byron pulled her back between two parked cars.

And then he saw it. The window on the passenger side rolling down just a fraction. Byron saw the gun barrel as it emerged. The overhead lighting bounced off the gray metal, creating a burst of illumination.

"Duck!" Byron cried as he threw her down to the ground beside a BMW. In much less than a heartbeat, he'd covered her body with his own.

Kady knew the moment the bullet had struck. She'd felt it. It hadn't hit her. It had hit Byron. Byron's body jerked, then tensed as the bullet tore into him. Despite being wounded, he was on his feet almost immediately, his own weapon drawn and in his hand. He fired as the vehicle sped away, but it was already too far for him to hit.

Turning toward her, cursing his aim, he gruffly demanded, "You hurt?"

Kady quickly scrambled to her feet, horrified. She couldn't take her eyes away from the wound. "No, but you are." There was blood flowing from his shoulder, down the sleeve of his jacket.

He looked down, as if suddenly aware of the pain. "Damn, I really liked this jacket."

"I'll buy you another one," she said, mentally uttering a prayer of thanks that the bullet hadn't been a few inches to the left. "C'mon, I'll take you back inside."

Byron was busy scanning the area. He took one last look around and then, satisfied that the man or men in the car weren't returning for another go at them, awkwardly holstered his gun.

"No."

She stared at him, stunned. Wondering if she had heard correctly. The man needed medical attention. Didn't he know that? Macho only went so far. "What do you mean, no?"

Byron held his ground. He wasn't about to go back up to the hospital. He'd just spent the past ten hours there.

"It's a two-letter word, Kady." His voice was

even, trying not to give away the fact that his arm felt like it was slowly being set on fire. "I'd figure that someone as intelligent as you would know what it means."

She didn't have the patience for this. "Don't give me sarcasm. You're bleeding."

But he made no move to follow her as she started to lead the way. "Observant, too. No end to your talents, are there, Doctor?"

Kady pressed her lips together to keep back a terse, frustrated comment. If she yelled, he'd yell back and nothing would be settled. She tried logic. "You need to have that looked at and taken care of."

"So look at it and take care of it," he answered simply. "You're a doctor."

She was rapidly losing patience. The man wasn't making any sense. "Why are you being so stubborn?"

"I don't like having to wait around. We've been in this damn place long enough today." And then, because in an odd sort of way he didn't want her thinking he was just plain crazy, he said, "I don't like hospitals." He didn't add that every time he walked into an E.R., especially this E.R., memories of Bobby's last minutes came flooding back to him, assaulting him.

There was something in his eyes that told her there was more to it than that. More that he wasn't saying. And then she remembered. Remembered that his brother had died here. Was that what Byron remembered every time he walked in with her? The battle that had been lost?

She could empathize with him. She'd lost battles here herself, although never for someone close to her. But it hurt nonetheless. She thought of the young mother she'd tried vainly to save. "Then this assignment must be hell for you," she said quietly.

He looked over her head, afraid that if he made eye contact, something inside of him would rip open. "Yeah, it is."

Very gently, Kady drew the jacket from his arm. "Here, let me take a look at it." She saw him wince as the material moved against his skin. "You know it's okay to yell and curse."

"Thanks," he said with effort. "I'll save it up for when you really tick me off."

Ever the warrior. Shaking her head, Kady looked at the wound. It appeared that the bullet had gone straight through. Taking her handkerchief, she pressed it against the hole, then slipped the sleeve back on. "Hold your hand against it," she instructed, then added, "It's a flesh wound."

"That means you can take care of it." It wasn't a question.

"Yes, I can take care of it." She picked up her purse where she'd dropped it, then began to lead the way to his car. "We should report this to the police."

"Fine. Give your brother-in-law a call when we get home." He saw the disapproval in her face. He knew she wanted him to call the police now. "Look, there're three doctors in the apartment, counting you, the last time I looked. You have access to two active police detectives and one retired one. We take care of this wound and then we go from there, okay?"

Not okay, she thought. Still leading the way, Kady looked at him. She was beginning to understand. "You don't want the police in on this, do you?"

No, he didn't. He'd had enough of the police force to last him a lifetime. "They tend to gum things up," he answered. And he wanted to get hold of whoever had done this himself.

The only problem was, he didn't want to leave Kady unguarded. He decided to call in Mavis once they got back to her apartment and things had been squared away. He was lucky enough to have gotten part of the license plate number.

She didn't want to argue over the right thing to do. The *first* thing to do was to get his wound looked at. "We'll discuss it later," she told him. They'd arrived at his car. Byron started to reach for the driver's door. Kady immediately placed her body directly in front of it, blocking his access. "You're not driving." There was no room in her voice for argument.

He'd driven under worse conditions than this. And more than that, he didn't like being told what he could or couldn't do. His eyes narrowed.

"Why not?"

Exasperated, hands on her hips, Kady glared at him. "I'm not going to stand here, explaining to you why a wounded man shouldn't be behind the wheel of a car. Now, either get into the passenger seat, or I put a call in to hospital security and have them haul your butt off to the E.R. Take your pick."

Byron got in on the passenger side. The seat belt proved to be a problem.

Reaching for his seat belt, Kady put the metal tongue into the slot, then fastened her own. "Now shut up and sit tight," she ordered, starting up the car.

Kady pulled out of the space and flew up the winding ramp toward street level. Byron tensed, bracing his body against the seat. He discovered that he had other things to think about besides his injured pride. The good doctor drove like a NASCAR pro.

Chapter 15

"Now are you going to take this seriously?" Byron asked.

He was in the main bathroom, sitting on the edge of the tub. Kady had her medical bag opened on the counter and had begun cleaning his wound. She still wasn't happy about his refusal to be seen in the E.R.

"I have always taken medicine seriously." Finished with the cotton swab, she tossed it into the light-blue wastebasket and reached for the needle and thread she'd prepared.

"Kady—" There was a warning note in his voice.

About to start, she held the needle in one hand and looked at him. "You know, I'm not sure, but I think this evening's probably the first time you've used my name."

His scowl deepened. "No, it's not, and don't change the subject."

Her eyes crinkled as she smiled. "I like the way you say it."

He caught his breath as she took the first stitch. "Kady—"

"Yes, just like that."

She could feel him giving her one of those soul-penetrating looks and she knew that sooner of later she was going to have to address the subject in something other than a light manner. She wasn't sure what he wanted from her, but she could guess.

Taking another stitch, Kady dug in. "I'm not changing my mind about testifying against Nicholas Skourous."

It took effort not to tense his bicep as she slid the needle beneath his skin. He could feel his eyes watering. "No one's asking you to do that."

She drew the needle out neatly. "So what are you asking me to do?"

It was hard talking while she was sewing up his shoulder. He focused on sounding natural. "Be more careful. Don't take any unnecessary chances."

Okay, so now she knew where this was going. Kady shook her head. "I'm not going to stop going to the clinic."

She had a feeling that the loud huff that escaped

his lips had nothing to do with the needle she was sticking through his skin. "They can get to you more easily in a place like that."

"I have you," she remind him cheerfully. "I'm bulletproof."

His eyes narrowed as he tried to get a look at her face. Was she serious? "You wouldn't have been if I hadn't blocked that shot."

"Which is why you're my hero." She reached for the small scissors to cut the thread, then stopped for a moment, concerned. It was bad enough that she'd had to live through that just now. She didn't want word of this getting out. "This is between us, okay?" It was half a statement, half a plea. "Don't tell my parents or my sisters what happened."

A light came into his eyes as he looked up at her. "I wasn't planning on it—but if that's what it takes to keep you in line…" His voice trailed off, letting her fill in the blanks.

"I'm as in line as I'm going to be, Byron."

To punctuate her statement, she dramatically cut the thread.

Putting the scissors and needle down on the counter, Kady examined her handiwork closely. Her stitches were small, equal. In a word, perfect. She'd always had an aptitude for sewing wounds.

She pursed her lips, wondering how the stitches felt on his end. "Does it hurt very much? I can give you a shot to deaden the pain if you like."

"I have my own way of dealing with the pain," he told her. Before she could ask what that was, Byron wrapped his arms around her hips and brought her closer to him until she was leaning her body against him.

A smile pulled at her lips. Thoughts about how things could have gone tonight were set aside. There was no point in dwelling on the dark side. "Okay, but tonight you're going to lie back and let me do all the work."

"Work?" A hint of a smile curved his mouth. "Is that what you call it now?"

"Some work feeds the soul." God, but she was so relieved that he was all right. That the wound he'd sustained was only minor. If anything had happened to him because of her…

Releasing her, Byron rose to his feet, then draped his arm across her shoulders. "Okay, show me how you're going to do all the work."

"You asked for it," she laughed.

Every night for the next week, the ritual continued to be the same. Byron would have her remain by the front door while he methodically checked out the interior of the apartment, room by room. After the parking garage incident, he was more adamant than ever about her remaining poised to flee at the slightest sign that something was amiss.

His increased vigilance was beginning to make

her genuinely uneasy, genuinely nervous. Mentally she damned Nicholas Skourous not just for murdering Milos and Ari but for stealing her peace of mind.

Half the time the apartment was empty when she arrived. Natalya and Tania were either at the hospital or out socializing. The silence on those evenings, as she stood beside the front door, waiting for Byron to give her the "all clear," crept under her skin. Making her imagine all sorts of terrible things.

This wasn't like her.

Byron's pessimism was getting to her, Kady thought grudgingly as she stood now, waiting for him to come back into the living room. It was Friday and her sisters were both out.

There was a copy of the yellow pages opened on the coffee table. Natalya had probably left that there. Her older sister had asked her if she and Byron wanted to join her and Mike, but this was her afternoon for the clinic and she knew she wouldn't be back in time, so she'd passed on the invitation.

She wished now that she'd said yes.

Then the same thought that had been plaguing her the past few days rose again. Once the trial was behind her and the threat to her life a thing of the past, Byron would be gone.

As good as their lovemaking was—and it was very, very good—she didn't fool herself. Byron wasn't the kind of man who allowed himself to be

tied down. No strings, that had been the understanding.

God, but she wanted strings.

Funny what a difference a few weeks could
make. Once upon a time she couldn't see herself
with anyone forever. Now…now she was having
trouble coping with the thought that Byron wasn't
always going to be part of her life.

She wondered if there was a way to get the trial
postponed so that she could have him a little longer.

Stupid thought, she upbraided herself.

She glanced at her watch. She'd been standing
here for at least five minutes, waiting. What was
taking him so long?

"Byron, I know you like to be thorough, but this
is carrying things too far, even for you." He made
no response. Kady frowned. "Byron?"

Still nothing.

Knowing Byron, he was probably going to jump
out at her to show her just how vulnerable she was.
His orders were to remain by the door until he came
back. This was undoubtedly a test.

She raised her voice. "Very funny, Byron. You
can come out now."

He didn't answer.

The hell with the test. Abandoning her post by the
door, Kady dropped her bag on the floor, shed her
coat, leaving it on the coat rack and stepped out of
her shoes the way she did every night. Her feet were

killing her right now. Even the most comfortable shoes began to hurt after a while and these had stopped fitting that description about four hours ago.

Okay, now she was getting annoyed. Crossing to the living room, she called out, "Byron, answer me."

Kady stopped dead as a man she'd never seen before walked into the living room from the rear of the apartment. "He can't hear you right now. He's taking a nap in your room."

Her breath caught in her throat. The man was of average height and build. What wasn't average was the gun in his left hand. The barrel had a silencer attached. Just like the one that had been used on Milos.

Kady began to back away.

Never taking his eyes off her, the man continued moving until his back was to the front door. Blocking her escape.

She'd done exactly what Byron had warned her not to do. She hadn't fled at the first sign that something was wrong.

Her pulse accelerated. She was trapped.

"What have you done to Byron?" she demanded.

"Don't worry, he'd not dead. Yet. First things first, right?" Lean, dressed in black, the gunman's eyes held a dark gleam. "It won't hurt, I promise you." His nostrils flared a little as he appeared to contemplate her fate. "It's just like going to sleep."

He enjoyed this. Enjoyed killing. Oh God, was

he lying? Had he killed Byron? Frantically she tried to think. She felt as if her mind had shattered into a million tiny fragments.

"You don't want to do this."

The thin lips peeled back in an almost maniacal grin. "Oh, now, there's where you're wrong. I do. I do want to do this. I'm getting paid a lot of money to do this. Now we can do this the hard way or the easy way." He started advancing on her. "I'm supposed to make this look like an accident. If you make me shoot you, I'm going to have to burn down the building. Think of all those innocent lives that'll be sacrificed."

"Accident?" she echoed. Her head just refused to process his words.

"An overdose. Or, you could throw yourself from the window." He laughed, the sound shredding her nerves. "I'll leave it up to you. I like spontaneity." He raised his gun, aiming it at her. "C'mon, what'll be? Tick-tock, time's wasting."

"You're insane," she cried.

He shrugged. "Everyone has a flaw."

Still moving away, Kady stumbled against the coffee table. Looking down, she saw the yellow pages. Desperate, she grabbed the thick book and hurled it at her would-be killer with all her might. She managed to deflect his weapon, sending the gun flying, but not before the trigger had been jerked. The gun fired and a bullet went into the ceiling.

Her heart pounding, Kady took off, running to Tania's room. To the only room in the apartment that had access to the fire escape.

Her hand shook as she stopped long enough to lock the door behind her. She knew it wouldn't prevent the gunman from getting into the room, but she prayed it would buy her enough time to open the window and escape.

The moment she pushed the sash up far enough to let her get out, the cold January air enveloped her. She was shaking even harder than before as she made her way onto the fire escape.

Her fingers began to ache from the cold almost immediately. She clung to the railing as she flew down the wrought-iron stairs. The apartments she passed were dark. Was anyone home? She couldn't risk pausing and banging on a window. He'd catch up to her.

It was five flights to the street, and the fire escape stairs didn't go all the way down. Kady jumped. Landing awkwardly, she twisted her ankle. She gritted her teeth and ran down the alley.

The gunman was right behind her, barreling down the fire escape.

As she ran, Kady searched in vain for something to use as a weapon. A bat, a board, a discarded tire iron. *Something.*

"Give up," the gunman taunted. "It's a dead end. There's a dumpster at the other end of the alley and even if you crawl in, I'll find you. You're just making it hard on yourself."

He was gaining on her and he was right. There was no way out. But just as he reached her, he screamed in pain. The scream all but muffled the gunshot. He staggered, then caught himself before he fell.

Kady cringed, moving out of the way. The very next moment, the gunman was being spun around. Byron held him up just long enough to pull his own arm back and then punch him. Even wounded, he had a powerful right cross. As the gunman sagged, Byron hit him again. The man went down, bleeding. He managed to mumble a curse before he passed out cold.

Relieved, still shaking, Kady flung herself against Byron, wrapping her arms around him. She didn't bother holding back her tears. He was alive. The gunman hadn't killed him. Byron was alive.

"Are you all right?" she wanted to know, moving her head back to look at him. "I thought he killed you."

"No, but he hit me on the head with something. I think it was an elephant." He'd been blindsided when he'd walked into Kady's room. It was going to be a long time before he forgave himself for that. Gingerly he touched his forehead. There was blood on his fingers when he looked at his hand. "When I came to, all I could think of was that he was going to kill you."

Still holding on to Byron, she looked back at the man on the ground. "He would have, if you hadn't shot him first."

Byron shook his head. "I didn't."

Kady stared at him. She was positive that she'd heard a shot. And there was a pool of blood beneath the gunman. "But—I don't understand. If you didn't shoot him, who did?"

Byron shifted so that she could look back toward the fire escape. Standing one story up, she saw the gang member whose baby she had delivered last month.

"I've got a feeling he's been watching over you. Word travels on the street," Byron told her when she looked at him quizzically. "Maybe he heard that someone had put a contract out on you." He had a feeling that they might never get to the bottom of it. It didn't matter. All that mattered was that she was alive. "I take back what I said about the clinic." One arm around her shoulders, Byron raised his other hand, acknowledging the teen.

"Looks like you've got yourself a guardian angel."

Kady smiled as she looked up at Byron. "I already knew that."

There was no need for a trial.

Two days after the would-be killer was taken into custody, Lyle Corbett, the assistant district attorney Kady had met with to discuss what she had seen that fateful morning, called her on her cell just as she and Byron walked into her apartment.

Bryon watched her, alert the moment he heard her say the A.D.A.'s name.

"That's great news," she finally said. "Thank you for calling. Yes, me, too, under better circumstances, I hope. Goodbye." The call over, she closed her cell phone slowly. Afraid that she'd imagined what she'd just heard.

Byron peered at her face, trying to read her expression. "Bad news?"

"No. Good news." Kady tucked the phone back in her pocket. The numb feeling was beginning to recede. She raised her eyes to Byron's face. "That guy you caught the other night flipped on Nicholas Skourous. Skourous's lawyer advised him to take a plea. Life in prison with no hope of parole. He did. It took the death penalty off the table." She shook her head.

"What?"

"The guy said that Ari was in on it. He let Skourous in to kill Milos." She frowned. She would have never suspected the other bodyguard. "Skourous said he'd promised him shares in the company."

Bryon snorted. "Instead, he got a share of a bullet." He'd seen it happen time and again. There was no such thing as honor among thieves. Or killers, either.

Looking at Kady, he drew in a breath. "So, it's over."

The sentence played itself in her head. Over. It was finally over. She could hardly believe it. She wasn't a marked woman anymore. "Yes."

And he knew what that meant. He was free to go. To pick up the threads of his life. Funny, he'd expected to feel better about that than he did. He certainly hadn't expected the deadness he felt in the center of his soul. "I guess you won't be needing me anymore."

Kady felt as if something suddenly gripped her. "A lot you know," she murmured under her breath.

He looked at her. "What?"

She was about to say, "Never mind," then thought to herself that she might never get another opportunity to tell him what was on her mind. Never get to say anything to him. Knowing Byron, he could very well just disappear on her. There was nothing to keep him here now.

The thought of never seeing him again was unbearable.

"I'm going to miss you," she finally said, then added, "For a lot of reasons." When he looked at her quizzically, she said, "You made me feel safe."

Was that all? He shrugged her words away. "That's what a bodyguard is supposed to do."

Kady shook her head. He didn't understand. "No. You made me feel safe," she reiterated the words slowly, trying to get her meaning across. "Being with you made me feel safe."

And that was something very new to her. Men were always the opposite sex, the opposite gender. She'd never felt as if she was on the same side of the fence as the man she was with. But Byron was different. The circumstances had been different. He wasn't someone she was dating, he was someone she needed in her life. And that took the fear away.

Byron smiled, nodding. Beginning to understand. "I kind of liked having my own doctor at my disposal." He paused, looking for words. Feeling inadequate. He stumbled ahead. "Maybe you won't have to miss me."

Was he saying that she'd get involved with someone and forget him? Forget what they'd been through? Did he think she was that shallow? Or didn't he realize what he'd come to mean to her? "If you're not here, I will."

He shoved his hands deep into his pockets. "And if I am?"

She was trying to follow him, but she didn't want to put words into his mouth. "What are you saying?"

Byron blew out an impatient breath. Frustration fanned his temper. "Look, I'm not good with words."

That didn't let him off the hook, she thought. "Then grunt. Draw pictures. Do mime. But let me know what you're thinking."

He sighed, his frustration growing. But she was still waiting, so he tried again.

"I'm thinking that just because it's over doesn't mean we don't see each other anymore." Frowning, he looked away for a moment. Voicing his feelings had always made him feel like he was standing barefoot on hot sand. "Your father called me the other day."

"My father?" He'd never said a word to her about this before now. For that matter, neither had her father. Just what was going on? This didn't make sense. "Why would my father call you?"

Byron nodded. "He said that he knew once I stopped looking after you, I'd need a job. He offered me one with his security firm as soon as I'm free."

Her mother was behind this. She'd bet her last dollar on it. The woman's hobbies were cooking and meddling, not in that order. Still, she couldn't find it in her heart to be angry. Especially if Byron said yes.

"And you're okay with that?" She studied his face, searching for her own answers.

He tried to sound nonchalant. The truth of it was, he was more than okay with that. "Man's gotta do something with himself."

"I quite agree." It was hard keeping the grin from her lips, so she gave up. "What else would you like to do with yourself?"

His eyes met hers. He felt a surge inside. A good

surge. "I was thinking more along the lines of what you might like to do with me."

The man could bob and weave like a pro, but she needed to have him pinned down. Just once. "A whole list of things comes to mind. Classes in Conversational English would be at the top of that list."

She'd completely lost him. "What?"

She tried to make this as simple as possible. Because she needed to hear the right answer. "Byron, do you feel anything for me?"

His frown told her he thought it was a stupid question. "Of course I feel something for you."

He might think it was stupid, but she didn't. "Well then, why won't you tell me?"

"You're supposed to know."

Of all the dumb, male things to say. "How?" she pressed. "How am I supposed to know?"

He threw up his hands. "People in love are supposed to know things about each other, aren't they? Intuit things?"

She stared at him. "Back up, back up. In love? You're in love with me?"

He couldn't figure out if she was happy about that, or if he'd just made a gross miscalculation. "Why? Don't you want me to be?"

"Well yes, but I'd like to know it." Her expression softened. This was a man who was going to have to be led. She didn't mind. "Why didn't you say anything?"

He looked at her, mystified. "I just did."

And then she laughed. "Yeah, I guess you just did." She wound her arms around his neck. "And, for what it's worth, I love you, too."

Relief flooded through his veins. "It's worth a lot," he told her.

Her mouth curved impishly. "How much?"

Okay, enough was enough. "Woman, will you please shut up so I can kiss you?"

She grinned. "I can do that."

And she did.

And so did he.

* * * * *

Don't miss the next DOCTORS PULASKI
out February 2008
from Silhouette Romantic Suspense.

*Turn the page for a sneak preview
of the first book in the new miniseries*
DIAMONDS DOWN UNDER
from Silhouette Desire®,
VOWS & A VENGEFUL GROOM
by Bronwyn Jameson

*Available January 2008
(SD #1843)*

*Silhouette Desire®
Always Powerful, Passionate and Provocative*

Kimberley Blackstone didn't notice the waiting horde of media until it was too late. Flashbulbs exploded around her like a New Year's light show. She skidded to a halt, so abruptly her trailing suitcase all but overtook her.

This had to be a case of mistaken identity. Surely. Kimberley hadn't been on the paparazzi hit list for close to a decade, not since she'd estranged herself from her billionaire father and his headline-hungry diamond business.

But no, it was *her* name they called. *Her* face was the focus of a swarm of lenses that circled her like avid hornets. Her heart started to pound with fear-fueled adrenaline.

What did they want?

What was going on?

With a rising sense of bewilderment she scanned the crowd for a clue, and her gaze fastened on a tall, leonine figure forcing his way to the front. A tall, familiar figure. Her head came up in stunned recognition, and their gazes collided across the sea of heads before the cameras erupted with another barrage of flashes, this time right in her exposed face.

Blinded by the flashbulbs—and by the shock of that momentary eye-meet—Kimberley didn't realize his intent until he'd forged his way to her side, possibly by the sheer strength of his personality. She felt his arm wrap around her shoulder, pulling her into the protective shelter of his body, allowing her no time to object. No chance to lift her hands to ward him off.

In the space of a hastily drawn breath, she found herself plastered knee-to-nose against six feet two inches of hard-bodied male.

Ric Perrini.

Her lover for ten torrid weeks, her husband for ten tumultuous days.

Her ex for ten tranquil years.

After all this time, he should not have felt so familiar but, oh dear, he did. She knew the scent of that body and its lean, muscular strength. She knew its heat and its slick power and every response it could draw from hers.

She also recognized the ease with which he'd taken control of the moment and the decisiveness of his deep voice when it rumbled close to her ear. "I have a car waiting outside. Is this your only luggage?"

Kimberley nodded. "I assume you will tell me," she said tightly, "what this welcome party is all about."

"Not while the welcome party is within earshot. No."

Barking a request for the cameramen to stand aside, Perrini took her hand and pulled her into step with his ground-eating stride. Kimberley let him, because he was right, damn his arrogant, Italian-suited hide. Despite the speed with which he whisked her across the airport terminal, she could almost feel the hot breath of the pursuing media on her back.

This was neither the time nor the place for explanations. Inside his car, however, she would get answers.

Now that the initial shock had been blown away—by the haste of their retreat, by the heat of her gathering indignation, by the rush of adrenaline fired by Perrini's presence and the looming verbal battle—her brain was starting to tick over. This had to be her father's doing. And if it was a Howard Blackstone publicity ploy, then it had to be about Blackstone Diamonds, the company that ruled his life.

The knowledge made her chest tighten with a familiar ache of disillusionment.

She'd known her father would be flying in from Sydney for today's opening of the newest in his chain of exclusive, high-end jewelry boutiques. The opulent shopfront sat adjacent to the rival business where Kimberley worked. No coincidence, she thought bitterly, just as it was no coincidence that Ric Perrini was here in Auckland ushering her to his car.

Perrini was Howard Blackstone's right-hand man, second in command at Blackstone Diamonds, a legacy of his short-lived marriage to the boss's daughter. No doubt her father had sent him to fetch her; the question was *why?*

* * * * *

Get swept away down under with the glitz and glamour of the Blackstone empire as Kimberley tries to determine the real reason behind her "reunion" with Ric....

Look for VOWS & A VENGEFUL GROOM
by Bronwyn Jameson
in stores January 2008.